"Oh, Nell, I have heard the queerest tales!" said Lady Mab. "The whole countryside is abuzz with speculation! What do you think has happened to Marriot?"

Eleanor stood at her projecting oriel window, somberly looking out. "I do not know what to think, my dear, except that Marriot did not disappear by choice. I have not the most distant guess of where he may have gotten to, and it makes not the slightest difference how much I cudgel my brain! The fact is that he departed White's one night six months ago and never returned home. He simply vanished! Not even Bow Street has been able to trace him one step."

Strange Bedfellows

A NOVEL BY

Maggie MacKeever

FAWCETT COVENTRY • NEW YORK

STRANGE BEDFELLOWS

Published by Fawcett Coventry Books, CBS Educational and
Professional Publishing, a division of CBS Inc.

ISBN: 0-449-50292-9

Printed in the United States of America

First Fawcett Coventry printing: June 1982

10   9   8   7   6   5   4   3   2   1

CHAPTER ONE

It was late night when the hackney coach clattered to a weary halt in front of a very fine several-storied Elizabethan brick town house. Stiffly, a young lady descended from the carriage, took firm grip of her bulging portmanteau, glanced doubtfully at the turrets and chimneys and wonderful bay windows which rose the full height of Marcham Towers to just below the battlemented parapet, at the cold moonlight reflected in countless diamond-shaped windowpanes.

Brisk assault on the ancient timbered door brought forth a sleepy servant who admitted her to an entrance hallway with carved ceiling and marble chessboard floor, suits of armor and racks of spears upon the walls. The young lady gazed curiously about. Though she had known the March family forever, their country estates abutting upon her papa's own, this was her first visit to Marcham Towers. She followed the servant up a great staircase with carved balusters and newel posts, then waited as he knocked discreetly on a door. The portal swung open to reveal a slender chestnut-haired lady on whose endearingly irregular features was an anxious look. As her amber gaze lit upon the newcomer, she blinked. The anxious expression faded, to be replaced in turn by disappointment and bewilderment. "Why, Mab!" Lady March said at length.

"You thought I was Marriot," Lady Amabel responded wisely, as she shifted her portmanteau. "I didn't think of that, and very sorry I am for it, Nell, if you got your hopes up for naught." She craned her lovely little neck to peer into the room beyond. "I take it you've had no word from the rascal yet?"

Lady March stepped aside, gestured for the newcomer to enter, bade the servant fetch them refresh-

5

ment and Lady Amabel to make herself comfortable. "You do not wish to discuss Marriot in front of the servants," remarked Mab with her usual acumen, as she divested herself of her long-sleeved, high-necked sapphire velvet pelisse. "As though they have not noticed that he has failed for quite six months to come home! Oh, Nell, I have heard the *queerest* tales! The whole countryside is abuzz with speculation! What do *you* think has happened to Marriot?"

Eleanor stood at her projecting oriel window, somberly looking out. "I do not know *what* to think, my dear, except that Marriot did not disappear by choice— I have not the most distant guess of where he may have gotten to, and it makes not the slightest difference *how* much I cudgel my brain! The fact is that he departed White's one night six months ago and never returned home. He simply vanished! Not even Bow Street has been able to trace him one step."

"Bow Street!" Lady Amabel's shudder was prompted not wholly by pleasurable dismay upon hearing mentioned those relentless representatives of the law, but also by the chill temperature of Lady March's solar. Mab snatched up her pelisse and moved closer to the fireplace. "Oh, Nell!"

Lady March did not similarly suffer from the chill temperatures; foresight, and experience of drafty Marcham Towers, had inspired her to bundle up in a man's fur cloak of the same venerable vintage as the house. "We must be realistic," she said, as she joined Mab at the fireplace, where they presented a pretty study in contrasts. At thirty, Nell was tall and slender, her features rendered exquisitely patrician by their slight irregularity, her chestnut hair worn in classical coils from which a few errant curls escaped. Mab, just turned nineteen, was both less tall and less slender, a glorious young beauty with huge mischievous blue eyes and black hair cropped short and worn in artfully disheveled curls.

"Realistic?" echoed Lady Amabel, her blue eyes opened wide. "Nell! You don't think—"

6

"No, I don't!" interrupted Lady March, a trifle crossly. "Had Marriot been murdered, his body would have been found. And had he been abducted, we would have received a ransom demand. So it must be something else altogether that has caused his disappearance—though I freely admit I can't think *what!*"

Several possible explanations presented themselves to Lady Amabel as she gazed thoughtfully upon the chimney piece, which incorporated a carved scene of Diana bathing and a mantel frieze carved with monkeys, birds and beasts. "Well, we know Marriot isn't of unsound mind, so it isn't *that!* I do not mean to cast a blight upon your spirits, Nell, but have you considered that Marriot may have eloped?"

In response to this suggestion, Lady March looked crosser still. "Bosh!" she said.

Lady Amabel wrinkled her pretty nose, which was enchantingly retroussé. "I know it sounds like so much moonshine, and that you and Marriot always dealt together delightfully, but I have noticed that gentlemen sometimes *stray!* However, Marriot is *your* husband, so you must know him best." She frowned. "Was Marriot in his altitudes, I wonder? I do not mean to infer that he is a drunkard, because of course he isn't, but there is no denying he was prone to take some odd notions when a trifle foxed. *Is* prone to do so!" she quickly amended upon glimpsing her friend's face. "Depend upon it, we shall discover Marriot is merely indulging one of his whims."

Eleanor did not reply. Even under influence of the grape she doubted her husband would grow so very absentminded as to forget home and wife for six months on end. To her severe misgivings she did not give voice, the servant arriving at that moment with a light repast. Before departing, he built up the fire and lit additional candles. With gusto, the ladies fell to their midnight feast, Mab pausing between mouthfuls to cast curious glances around the room.

The solar must have changed little in the centuries of its existence, Lady Amabel thought, as she gazed upon the ceiling with its attractive symmetrical design culminating in several Tudor roses and the plaster frieze in which Diana, her dogs and attendants hunted stags and elephants and lions in a forest of trees. The framework of the wainscoting was painted brilliant red with touches of blue and gold. Even the furnishings were Elizabethan, including a counting table with a checkered top, chairs embroidered with flowers and leaves and fruits, and stools upholstered with green velvet and studded with nails.

While her visitor thus indulged herself, Lady March withdrew to the daybed where she'd been huddling when Lady Amabel arrived, reading an edifying work entitled *The History of Serpents,* which solemnly stated that dragons are wont to hunt elephants in packs. Nell's own curious gaze moved from Mab to her bulging portmanteau, which had been abandoned just inside the door. "You have not told me what you are doing here."

Cautiously, Lady Amabel eyed her hostess, who at times could be a very high stickler. "Goose!" she said merrily. "I have come to bear you company in your lonely vigil. What are friends *for?*"

That it had taken her friend six months to come to her assistance Lady March did not point out. "But it is so very late," she said.

"Yes, but that is not *my* fault." Replete, Mab brushed crumbs off the skirt of her white muslin gown. "I came in a nightcoach, and then a hackney, and *such* an adventure it was!"

The details of that adventure Nell could well imagine, Mab being the sort of young lady whose life was never dull. "You didn't travel here alone! Your papa—"

"My papa," interrupted Lady Amabel, with grim voice and irately sparkling eye, "is a cruelly unfeeling *beast!* He is curst high-handed—certainly he has tried *my* civility too high! And it is never the least use disputing with him because he doesn't *listen*—well! I thought that since I am fated to be melancholy, there is no one I would rather be melancholy with than *you!*"

Foreseeing a dramatic exchange of confidences, Lady March attempted to settle herself more comfortably among the myriad embroidered cushions upon the daybed, which was made of oak painted a chocolate red and ornamented with floral arabesques, its two paneled ends angling stiffly outward. "Thank you!" she said drily. "I hesitate to point out that I already have Cousin Henrietta to bear me company."

"Your Cousin Henrietta," Lady Amabel responded bluntly, "is less likely to elevate your spirits than plunge you smack into the dumps! Never have I known so dismal a female. No wonder you are so pulled-about."

This intelligence that she was not at her best Lady March accepted philosophically. Not only was Nell without vanity, in the eye of other than her vanished husband she cared not how she looked. "I would just as soon *not* have Henrietta," she confessed, casting the closed door a guilty look. "She was wished upon me by my family. But you will not lead me up the garden path so easily as that, my dear! I think I need to know what—other than a hackney coach!—has brought you to me in the dead of night." She cast a pointed glance at the bulging portmanteau. "Am I to conclude you mean to stay?"

"Well, er, yes." Lady Amabel had the grace to look abashed. "I truly *have* come to be with you in your hour of need, Nell—if you should not object!"

Lady March pulled her fur cloak closer and ruefully regarded her young friend. Amabel's expression was guileless. More to the point, her pretty nose, framed so becomingly by her tucked silk bonnet with lace frills and ribbon bowknot, was red. "Poor child, you're freezing!" cried Nell, as she rose to ring for her sleepy servant and request that a room be made up for her guest. "Come closer to the fire. You may not wish to stay with me when you discover how cold is this old mausoleum of a house. It is full of the oddest drafts—due to the secret passages, I suppose."

"Secret passages?" echoed Mab, big eyes opened

wide, as she joined Nell at the fireplace. "You're bamming me."

"No such thing, I promise you; Marcham Towers was in the possession of a Catholic family during the Civil Wars. We have a priest hole and a hidden attic and two secret passages that I know of. There is rumored to be an entrance in this very room, but I don't know where. Marriot would. Unfortunately we cannot ask him." Here Lady March's composure deserted her. "Oh, Mab! I have been teasing myself with thoughts of all the dreadful things that might have happened to him, and it upsets me dreadfully, and yet I cannot think what to *do!*"

"There, there!" soothed Lady Amabel, whilst reflecting it was extremely awkward to try and comfort someone considerably taller than oneself. "You have been dwelling too much on it! Not that you *shouldn't* think about Marriot—gracious, how could you *not* wonder what the blazes he is up to! You would wonder even more had you not stayed here in London, because there was *such* talk. One contingent even had it that Marriot had run afoul of the spies of that fiendish Frenchman— the Serpent of Corsica! The Fiend of the Bottomless Pit! Not that *I* believed such stuff for a minute, no, nor anyone else, despite all these invasion scares. But there is something very queer about it, Nell. Even Papa said Marriot's disappearance was too smoky by half." A trifle belatedly, it occurred to Lady Amabel that this was no cheerful choice of topic. "Anyway, now that I am with you, you may think about *my* troubles, which will be an excellent antidote for *your* distress!"

The suspicion that her vanished husband might have fallen victim of some devilish stratagem had also crossed Lady March's mind. It was not a thought that she wished to long entertain. "You have not told me what your troubles *are,*" she gently pointed out. "You and your papa have had a difference of opinion, I conclude—but *why?*"

In response to this not unreasonable question, Lady Amabel abandoned her rôle of comforter for one of a damsel in sore need of being soothed herself. "Oh, Nell! Papa has said I may not marry Fergus!" she wailed, and burst into gusty tears.

"Fergus?" echoed Eleanor, as she enfolded Mab also in her huge fur cloak and allowed the damsel to weep all over her silk gown. It was not the first time during the several years of their acquaintance that Nell had thus provided comfort to the motherless and highly volatile Amabel. "Who is this Fergus, pray?"

"Nell, could you but see him!" Lady Amabel raised a countenance as bedazzled as if her beloved were indeed within her sight. "Fergus has *everything* prime about him! He is a gentleman of substance, a veritable Adonis, a *particularly* elegant, handsome man! *All* that I could wish!"

"Then wherein lies the problem?" Lady March suspected her young friend was fashioning mountains out of molehills, and not for the first time. Amabel possessed a keen sense of the dramatic, as perhaps need not be explained. "Surely your papa must approve this paragon."

"He must, must he?" Mab's blue eyes flashed, and her delicious lip curled. "You would think so! You would think that any father with an *ounce* of human feeling would not deny his only daughter the gentleman upon whom her heart was set—especially when that gentleman is handsome as Adonis, and rich as Croesus, and a baron to boot—but not Papa! Fergus spoke to him very properly. Do you know what Papa said when he was made aware that I was being offered a highly flattering alliance? *Do* you, Nell?"

Fascinated, Lady March gazed upon her friend's indignant features. "Tell me!" she begged.

"He said that I was a little zany, and Fergus a dandified popinjay!" Mab's lower lip trembled. "Oh, *bother* the man! Sometimes I wish I were an orphan, although I am sure no girl could be fonder of her papa than I am. But how *dare* he speak to Fergus in such a disrespectful manner—to say nothing of the cruel way in which he has used me!" She sniffled. "My case is truly desperate!

11

Now you see why I am grown so melancholy, dear Nell, and why I have come to you. Together we shall endeavor to bear with resignation our irreparable losses!"

Though Lady March had been trying very hard for the past six months *not* to believe that her loss was irreparable, she was not so poor-spirited as to point this out. It was almost as good as a play to see Mab enact a Cheltenham tragedy. However, since the hour grew ever later, and her eyelids accordingly heavy, Nell deemed it time the curtain descend. "You have been wrested from your lover's arms," she said sympathetically. "Poor Amabel."

Paradoxically in a young lady so inclined to the dramatic, Mab was also very honest. "Er, not exactly," she admitted, pink of cheek. "Though I very *nearly* was, because Fergus cut up so stiff at being called a popinjay. And so he should have, poor lamb, because he *isn't*, Nell, I promise you." She lowered her eyes. "But I shall leave you to judge *that* for yourself!"

"Will you?" As the result of a pang of premonition, Eleanor looked severe. "How is that, miss?"

Mab's cheeks turned even pinker. "I daresay Fergus will call on you, once he discovers I'm in town."

"Mab!" Eleanor's voice was stern. "What will your father say to *that*, do you think?"

"Nothing, I hope, since he won't know about it!" Looking irresistibly earnest, Mab clutched Lady March's hands and gazed pleadingly up into her face. "Nell, I suspect you won't like this above half, but I have run away from home."

"Run away—" Words failed Eleanor. As if it were not trial enough that Marriot had disappeared, victim of some wicked fate upon the precise gruesome nature of which Cousin Henrietta speculated a good twenty hours of each day, now Nell must anticipate the momentary descent of Mab's father's wrath upon her head. Mab's sire was gentle neither of tongue nor temper. "You *wretched* child!" Nell sighed.

But Mab was not attending to her strictures, nor trying to disarm. Instead she was gazing in an astonished manner at the wall behind Lady March. Puzzled, Eleanor glanced over her shoulder. She, too, stared as a portion of the wainscoting swung silently away.

Through the opening stepped a disheveled masculine figure. He straightened and stood blinking in the candlelight. No damsel with a sense of the dramatic could forego such an opportunity. "It's a ghost!" shrieked Lady Amabel, with relish, and fainted dead away.

CHAPTER TWO

Why Lady Amabel should swoon upon sight of him, Lord March could not guess. In fact, there were any number of points upon which Lord March was uncertain, among them why he should be entering his own house via a secret passage, clutching to him a shabby valise, in the dead of night. Anticipating enlightenment, he glanced hopefully at his wife. But Eleanor, too, surprised him, not in the keen rush of pleasure he experienced at sight of her, because there was to Marriot no more pleasurable sight existent than his countess, with her amber eyes and faintly aquiline features and heavy chestnut hair, but she was not accustomed to stare at him in such an owlish manner, as if he was the last person she expected.

He set down the valise. "Hallo, puss! You look surprised to see me."

"Surprised!" As if released by his words from a trance, Lady March flew straight into her husband's arms. "Marriot, you *wretch!* I am so prodigious glad you have come home! Oh, *where* have you been?"

Lord March was not the least bit reluctant to be passionately embraced, and responded with equal fervor to his wife's caress. Oddly, it felt as though a great deal of time had elapsed since last he had engaged in such delightful husbandly pursuits. Apparently he was more in love with his wife than ever, decided Marriot, then abandoned that confusing speculation—for he had hitherto thought that man could never adore woman more than he adored his Nell—for the greater satisfaction of raining kisses upon her cheek and throat and brow. Because Lady March enjoyed receiving her husband's salutes as much as he enjoyed presenting them, and initiated further such activities in her own

14

turn, it was many moments later when they resumed speech. That they did so at this point was due only to a mutual discovery of the need to draw breath. As he did so, Lord March gazed in a fond fashion upon his wife's face, which he held cupped between his palms. "Nell! You are crying!" he observed, dismayed.

"Naturally I am crying!" Lady March wiped her face on the sleeve of her dress. "You have been gone so long! Oh, Marriot, are you *truly* here? I cannot believe that you have at last returned."

"Of course it is truly me." Lord March's devotion to his wife was not lessened by her occasional tendency to talk nonsense. In proof of that devotion, he drew her close against him, her chestnut hair against his chest. "Who else would it be, little goose? And I am glad you've missed me, although I've only been to White's. Come to think on it, I've missed you too!" Nell drew back to gaze searchingly up at him. What disturbed her, Marriot could not fathom. With tender fingers he tilted up her chin and diverted her attention with an extremely ardent kiss. Nell made a little noise deep in her throat and flung her arms around Marriot's neck. In so doing, her fingers encountered a lump on the back of his skull. The hair around that lump was damp and matted. Amorous intentions abandoned Lord and Lady March in the same moment. "Marriot, you're hurt!" cried Nell. His lordship merely winced.

Closer inspection revealed that the injury was not serious, merely an egg-shaped swelling, apparently the result of some recent sharp blow. "Damned if I can explain it!" responded Marriot when questioned as to the injury's source. Gingerly he fingered his sore head and sat down on the pillow-strewn daybed. "I seem to recall being set upon by footpads."

"Footpads! Marriot!" Eleanor, who had not yet recovered from the shock of her husband's abrupt reappearance, dropped down before him on her knees. "You could have been killed! Indeed, I feared you *had* been. There was a rumor that you had run afoul of Napoleon's agents. There was even a suggestion that you might have eloped."

"*Eloped?*" Lord March spoke absentmindedly, his attention on settling his wife and her voluminous fur cloak comfortably on his lap. "Why the deuce should I do such a cork-brained thing as that?"

Nell leaned back against her husband's shoulder. "I believe the theory was that you might have shot the cat. Don't scowl at me, Marriot; it wasn't *my* suggestion! You cannot deny that you have grown a trifle absent-minded on various occasions when you have imbibed a trifle too much."

To these wifely strictures upon the subject of strong drink, Lord March responded with unimpaired good humor, perhaps because between strictures his wife was nibbling on his ear. "I'd have had to be drunk as a wheelbarrow to forget I was mad for *you*, puss!" he said frankly, and then several kisses later added, "There! You'll know better than to think such a thing again."

"But I *didn't* think it!" With icy fingers, Lady March stroked her husband's lean face. "It was Mab."

"Mab?" Lord March caught his wife's cold hand and warmed it with his breath. In so doing, he glimpsed Lady Amabel, sprawled gracefully upon the floor. "Should we try and revive her, do you think?"

Eleanor glanced over her shoulder at her uninvited guest. "Leave her!" Nell said callously. "She looks comfortable enough, and she's too close to the fire to take chill. Oh, Marriot, I have been in *such* a pucker! I had begun to wonder if you would *never* return!"

Why his usually level-headed countess had suddenly taken such a bird-witted notion, Lord March could not imagine, but he was not slow to set her fears at rest. Another lengthy interlude followed, the mood shattered only when Marriot abruptly raised his head to frown at Lady Amabel's inert figure. "What's this about a ghost? Why should Mab swoon at sight of me? The brat has known me all her life."

16

Nell sighed. Explanations were in order. "What do you expect after an absence of six months?"

"Six months!" Lord March stared disbelieving at his countess. "You jest!"

"No, she doesn't!" Stiffly, Lady Amabel rose. While she had been quite content to be as one senseless whilst Lord and Lady March conducted their reunion, Mab was relieved to remove herself at last from the hard, cold, and exceedingly *un*comfortable floor. "You have been missing for quite that long, Marriot, and I wish you would tell us what the blazes you have been about." In eager anticipation of his answer, Mab perched upon an embroidery-covered chair.

Lord March's answer was not swift in coming, was so very tardy that Mab had ample time to inspect the lush plant life of the chair upon which she sat—roses and daisies and strawberry blossoms, leaves and fruit—and to discover a caterpillar worked cunningly into the design. "I wish you two would stop cuddling!" she said crossly, glancing up from her inspection of the chair to discover Lord and Lady March gazing rapt into each other's eyes. "While I am glad to learn that *some*one has been made heart-whole again, the sight of the pair of you hanging upon one another's lips and swearing eternal devotion makes me wish to gnash my teeth! I'm beginning to think that Papa was right; there *is* something dashed smoky about your disappearance, Marriot. Do you mean to tell us you *don't* know you were missing? And why did you feel obliged to use a secret passage to enter your own house?"

"I don't know." Lord March released his wife to rub his temples, as if by that simple expedient memory might be restored. It was not. "The last I recollect is leaving White's and being set upon by footpads—though I'm damned if I know if I was set upon then, or tonight." He touched his wound, and grimaced. "Or both!"

"Oh!" gasped Nell, concerned. "You *are* hurt! I will send for some hot water—"

"No!" Mab interrupted firmly, thus demonstrating

17

that she was the only occupant of the solar who had not temporarily set aside her good sense. *"Think,* Nell! Marriot has no explanation of his six-month absence, and returns home like a thief in the dead of night—it looks very much to me like there's something very havey-cavey going on here, and until we are certain that there *isn't,* Marriot's presence had much better not be broadcast."

"Havey-cavey!" Upon this slight to her miraculously restored husband, Lady March's bosom swelled. "How *dare* you suggest such a thing, Mab? And after we have taken you in!"

"I'm not suggesting anything, but telling you what other people may think." Lord March appeared a great deal more interested in his wife's swelling bosom than his own dire predicament, Mab thought. She wrinkled her nose. "You have been *some*where for the past six months. In a stable, from the smell and look of you!" Lord March wrinkled his own nose, sniffed and looked appalled.

"Never mind!" Eleanor didn't mind the smell of horses and was so glad to have her husband restored that she wouldn't have minded if he'd smelled much worse. Prompted by Lady Amabel's ominous hints, Nell drew back to take a good look at her spouse. He looked little different than he had six months past, she decided as she gazed upon his angular, mobile, utterly charming face. Marriot was not especially handsome, but possessed a magnetism that rendered mere good looks superficial. There were minor alterations; always athletic, Marriot was thinner than Nell remembered. His dark hair was longer than it had been six months past, and was currently as disheveled as any fashionable gentleman might achieve after hours spent before a looking glass. The most startling difference was in his clothing: knee breeches and unpolished boots and a simple white shirt open at the throat. However, there was no alteration whatsoever in the fond expression in his green eyes. "Darling!" murmured Nell huskily, as she lifted her fingers to trace the outline of his lips.

"Ahem!" interjected Lady Amabel, causing and Lady March to look at her askance. "It is that you are so pleased to be reunited, but don think it would be wise if we were to expend some thought upon what Marriot has been about? You don't realize what a sensation you created by disappearing, Marriot. People are naturally going to be very curious, even more curious than I—and much less inclined to believe that you don't know where you've been, or what you've been doing for six months." Pointedly, she regarded Eleanor, settled so comfortably upon his lordship's lap. "I do not mean to be a spoilsport, but perhaps if you were to apply your mind, you might recall."

Lord March's reflections during the moments since his emergence from the secret passage had had little in them of anything but his wife. Amabel's arguments were not without merit. Reluctantly, he set Nell off his lap and beside him on the daybed. As he did so, his hand brushed against the book she had been reading and knocked it to the floor. He picked it up. *The History of Serpents?*" he ironically inquired.

Nell took the book. "Nothing is worse for a dragon's digestion than apples," she remarked. "I have been reading all manner of strange things these past months, Marriot, while praying you would return."

Marriot was coming to accept the fact of his long absence; his wife looked as delectable to him as a feast must to a starving man. "Eleanor, forgive me!" he begged, enfolding her in his arms.

"Anything!" gasped Nell, breathless.

"Oh, the devil!" muttered Mab, as Lord and Lady March again embraced. Such obvious, uninhibited affection was enough to cast a less fortunate maiden into the dismals. Not that Mab begrudged her friends their happiness, even though it quite wrung her heart with envy. Her papa was the most heartless wretch in nature to forbid her such happiness of her own. A popinjay! One could not blame Fergus for keenly feeling such rudeness.

Lady Amabel's father claimed she was fit for some-

19

...ing better, but Mab seriously doubted whether something better existed than the well-heeled and well-situated, perfectly correct and unassuming and gloriously handsome Baron Parrington. Perhaps Marriot might be persuaded to put in a good word for Fergus with her papa? It was a consideration. This was no moment to intrude the topic, judging from the lack of attention which Lord March awarded the much more pressing question of where he'd spent the last six months. Mab cast his lordship and his lady an envious, exasperated glance. Then her gaze fell upon his shabby valise. Perhaps therein lurked a clue as to his recent whereabouts. Mab rose from her chair, grasped the valise and deposited it at—and inadvertently upon—Lord March's feet.

Thus recalled to his surroundings, Marriot awarded Lady Amabel an ungrateful frown. "Limb of Satan!" he remarked. "Will it satisfy you if I vow upon my solemn word of honor that I don't know *where* I've been? *Now* will you go to bed so that Nell and I may, er, talk privately?" He winked at his countess. "We have a lot of catching up to do."

"How I missed you, Marriot!" responded Lady March with her endearingly crooked smile. "But Mab is right, as usual—even if her papa *has* accused her of acting like a loony! We must apply ourselves to this puzzle of where you've been. It will be the first question Cousin Henrietta asks upon discovering you've returned, and you may be sure that whatever you tell her will be speedily spread all about the town. Even if you cannot remember, we must have some story ready, I think."

"Cousin Henrietta!" Lord March's mobile features wore a look of keen distaste. "You cannot mean to tell me that wretchedly interfering female is in this house."

"I am afraid so. She descended upon me immediately she heard of your disappearance, and has had me cudgeling my brain as to how I may be rid of her ever since."

"The deuce!" muttered Lord March bitterly. Withstanding the temptation to cradle her husband's mistreated head against her breast, Nell turned away. Her reflection in the oriel window caused her another, wryer smile. How carefully she had dressed in this lilac silk gown with white satin sleeves, and edged with lace, as she had dressed countless other nights, on the slender chance that Marriot might come home. This night he *had* returned, to find her rumpled and disheveled from the heavy cloak, her gown stained with Mab's copious tears. Not that he had seemed to mind. Eleanor turned back to gaze dotingly upon her spouse. *How* she loved the man.

That glance Mab intercepted, as well as the keen manner in which Lord March returned it; hastily, she cleared her throat. "Mayhap," she suggested, "we may find an answer to the mystery in Marriot's valise. I'll just open it, shall I?" She suited action to words. Then her blue eyes opened wide, and her pretty lips formed a perfect O. "Coo!" she said.

'Coo'? Lady March was very curious as to what had inspired her friend to make noises like a chambermaid. She, too, approached the valise. Her amber eyes also widened. "The devil!" she breathed.

By the conduct of his companions, Marriot's own interest was aroused. He lowered his fond gaze from his wife's startled face to the contents of the valise. By the sight that there greeted him, Lord March was bereft of speech. Mab brought forth a candelabra. Twinkling in the soft light were countless expensive jewels. Emeralds and rubies, diamonds and pearls—"Good God!" he said at last.

Lady Amabel plunged reckless fingers into the valise, held up an enormous diamond, cut as a rose, in a simple gold setting with a hanging pearl. In quick succession she brought forth a bracelet set with diamonds, emeralds and rubies in enameled gold; a brooch composed of a diamond spray of leafy flowers set in silver; a parure of rubies and emeralds. Then she looked quizzically at Marriot. "I did not think you would go *this* far," Mab murmured. "Even in your altitudes!"

21

"In my—" Lord March's blank expression changed to consternation. "You don't think I *stole* these things?"

"What else *can* we think?" Mab dropped the jewels back into the valise and closed it. "Whether you stole the jewels or not, you are in possession of them, and therefore in the devil of a fix."

Eleanor stirred. "No! Marriot could not do such a thing. I forbid you to even *think* it, Mab!"

"But we *must* think about it, puss!" Lord March gently pointed out. "Having the things, we must decide what to do with them—unfortunately, one cannot just toss such expensive baubles aside." His own smile, as he studied his wife, was crooked. "This is a pretty pickle! You will be sorry I have come home."

"Never, Marriot!" Eleanor was less stricken by the suggestion that her husband might have engaged in skulduggery than by his obvious distress. "I would not care if you robbed the—the Bank of England! And I know very well you didn't, or anyone else." She hugged him. "It is very late and we are all very weary! Things will seem less difficult in the morning. I suggest we retire."

"An excellent idea." Lord March put his wife away from him, picked up the valise, and approached the wainscoting. "I will take up residence in the attics until we have determined what must be done."

"In the *attics?*" Lady March was saddened that her husband's long-awaited homecoming should end on so sour a note. "Then I will come with you, Marriot."

To turn down so generous an offer when in sore need of his wife's companionship was the act of a true nobleman. Noble Lord March was, whether or not he had recently taken up burglary as a sideline. "No," he said firmly. "Not until this mystery is cleared up. I would not have you waste yourself, my darling, on a man who may be a common thief—or worse!" So saying, he stepped back through the wainscoting. The panel swung shut.

CHAPTER THREE

If Lord and Lady March were less than thrilled with the puzzle into which they had been so abruptly plunged, Lady Amabel was enthusiastic enough for all three. She did not like to see her friends made miserable, but the energy required to amend this topsy-turvy situation must very effectively distract a damsel from her own sore heart. Not that Mab's heart was *broken*, precisely, it was merely severely wrenched. Nor did she despair of persuading her papa of the injustice he had done her. How this miracle might be accomplished she was not yet certain, but trusted enlightenment would come.

These optimistic reflections having occupied her until she arrived at her destination, Mab paused outside the door of Lord and Lady March's bedchamber, hand upraised to knock. Faintly from within came voices. Had Marriot overcome his foolish scruples? Unhesitant, Mab pressed her dainty ear to the door. Those peevish tones definitely did not belong to Lord March; were indeed gloomily prophesying his lordship's fate. "Perhaps," said Cousin Henrietta as Mab entered, "he has been taken by a press gang!"

"Moonshine!" commented Lady Amabel with all the self-assurance of a young lady to whom nothing save the object of her girlish dreams had ever been denied. "If this is the way you have been going on, Henrietta, it is no wonder poor Nell has fallen into a melancholy. We must try and elevate her spirits, not cast them down!"

Upon being interrupted in mid-lament, the object of Lady Amabel's strictures blinked and stared. Cousin Henrietta was a short, plump, wispy white-haired female midway through her fifth decade. Her round face might have been attractive had it not been marred by lines of discontent. "Lady Amabel!" she tittered. "I did not expect—that is, how do *you* come to be here?"

"By coach, how else?" Frankly curious, Mab gazed about her. The bedroom was charming, incorporating a small fireplace decorated with imported colored marbles, small mullioned windows with lozenge-shaped panels and ancient soft green glass, plaster walls painted in brilliant shades of greens and reds, yellows and blues, and featuring a running design of humans and animals amid a large quantity of leaves. "Like you, I have come to be with Nell in her hour of need."

The irony of this statement—Henrietta served no needs but her own—the older woman let pass. She clasped her hands to her plump bosom encased in an unhappy shade of puce. "Poor, *poor* Eleanor!" she cried. "I have been endeavoring to discover just *why* Marriot may have left in so clandestine a fashion. Are you *certain,* Eleanor, that you and he did not have a falling-out?"

Having completed her inspection of the chamber, Mab turned toward the huge four-poster bedstead which stood on a dais at one end of the room. From the depths of the formidably carved structure came a single word. The tone in which the word was spoken was irritable. The word was "Poppycock!" In less hostile accents the speaker added, "Come here and sit by me, Mab, and share my chocolate! Perhaps between us we may persuade Henrietta that Marriot has *not* stuck his spoon in the wall."

Lady Amabel was not slow to accept this invitation; her stylish high-necked morning dress with tucks around the hem was not designed for arctic temperatures, and Mab was shivering despite her shawl. The bedroom was very cold, Cousin Henrietta's bulk absorbing the large portion of the fire's warmth.

"I did not say Marriot had 'stuck his spoon in the wall,' as you so inelegantly phrase it," that worthy protested, while with a disapproving expression she watched Lady Amabel climb onto the huge bed. In spite of her

24

efforts at comfort and consolation Henrietta had never received so hospitable an invitation from the bed's occupant and was consequently feeling very ill-used. "I only seek to prepare you for what I fear must be a very unpleasant event. We must face facts! Were Marriot able, he would have long since sent us word." Meaningfully, she hesitated. "Providing, that is, that he *wished* to."

Mab had paused to admire the hangings of the ancient bed, white linen embroidered in red and blue and green silks. The glance she awarded Henrietta was a great deal less appreciative. "Are you hinting that Marriot has developed petticoat-fever, ma'am? I think you must *want* to see Nell in the pathetics! It is nonsense anyway, because Marriot would have to be drunk as a wheelbarrow to give another female a second glance, and he isn't addicted to the bottle, so there!" She disappeared from view. "I daresay we shall have word of him any day."

Henrietta frowned at the bedstead; unless she was very much mistaken, she had just been given a sharp set down by a most impertinent chit. Lady Amabel had no proper way of thinking, else she would not speak so rudely to her elders. But Henrietta had known for years that Mab was a hoyden and a madcap, a sad romp upon whose unseemly spirits a check should have been imposed. Unfortunately, Mab's father did not adhere to Henrietta's belief that young ladies should look very demure and never say a word.

Henrietta's own voice betrayed none of her chagrin. "I am very much afraid that any word we have of Marriot must be unhappy at this point, and so I have warned Eleanor. She will not heed my advice, unfortunately. Perhaps you may help me persuade her that she must prepare herself to receive very bad news, Lady Amabel."

What Eleanor was prepared to do was throttle her cousin, thought Mab, a sentiment which she heartily endorsed. "But I don't think she *will* receive bad news," Mab responded, nudging Nell, who was staring mur-

25

derously at an intricately carved bedpost. "I've the *oddest* notion that Marriot will turn up any day."

Had she heard Eleanor *laugh?* wondered Henrietta, eyeing the four-poster. Surely not! "I hope we may not have Marriot brought to us with his *toes* turned up! You do not perceive the evils that await the unwary, Lady Amabel. There are ugly customers in the world, and devilry afoot. Look at Bonaparte—I mean, I hope we shall not *have* to look at him, but I wouldn't count on it! I have heard that he has under construction a monstrous bridge by which his troops will pass from Calais to Dover, directed by officers in air balloons; and also that a Channel tunnel is being engineered by a mining expert. Mark my words, we shall all awaken one morning to find we have been murdered in our beds!"

The bed upon which Lady Amabel currently reclined was very comfortable, even though its owner was in possession of all the blankets and was trying so hard to contain an untimely onslaught of giggles that the whole structure shook, not to mention the lavish lace which trimmed her huge, absurdly flattering nightcap. "I am not certain who you expect to murder us," Lady Amabel remarked. "Marriot or Bonaparte? This is a very foolish conversation. Marriot has come to no harm." She nudged the giggling Nell. "I feel it in my bones!"

All that Cousin Henrietta felt in *her* bones was a continuous dull aching, the result of being confined during inclement weather in this drafty old mansion. Henrietta was not among the numerous admirers of Marcham Towers. Those individuals with a passion for antique architecture and furnishings might alter their opinions, she thought sourly, if obliged to winter in the house. Not that Henrietta was *obliged* to do so, save by her sense of duty, which was almost as strong as her fondness for prying into the intimate details of other people's lives. Henrietta was not a prattle-bag precisely, but was more a parasite. She was positively agog to learn why Lord March had deserted his lady. Now

Lady Amabel had appeared on the scene to distract Eleanor just when Henrietta had been in momentary expectation of becoming her confidante. It was very bad. "You cannot be certain to what lengths Marriot may have been drawn," she ominously remarked.

Having wrested from her hostess a fair share of the blankets and accepted from her a cup of rapidly cooling chocolate, Mab was very luxuriously disposed. Again she nudged Eleanor. "That is very true," Mab responded solemnly. "I have already considered that Marriot might have run afoul of Bonaparte's agents—perhaps even the Mad Corsican himself! I have heard it said that Bonaparte has disguised himself as a British sailor and is patrolling English shores at night aboard a fishing smack! Women should be allowed to join the militia, I think. *We* would not fire the beacons by mistake. But if not by Bonaparte's agents, perhaps Marriot has been abducted by some other fiendish sort. Perhaps even tinkers! Although I do not know why they should abduct a grown man in the heart of London—but one never knows with that low, vulgar sort!"

Henrietta primmed her lips. "You mock me, miss, and you should not; age is the best advisor of youth. Moreover, horrid things *do* happen in London, as you would know if you read the newssheets. Just the other day Lady Nelson was set upon by footpads, and relieved of her jewels and purse, in broad daylight!" Her expression grew suspicious. "In truth, I am surprised that your father took no better precautions for *your* safety. You were not here yesterday and yet are here this morning, and therefore must have arrived in the middle of the night."

Though Mab could not see Henrietta due to the intricate carvings and enveloping draperies of the bed, she heard the curiosity in her voice. "I was in no danger!" Mab responded serenely. "You may trust Papa for that. Enough about my travels! Now that I am come to bear you company, how do you propose to entertain me, Nell?"

27

"Entertain you?" All merriment had abandoned Lady March upon mention of footpads.

"Entertainment!" Upon hearing this shocking suggestion, Henrietta was hard put to maintain a semblance of civility. "Marriot is missing and you talk of *entertainment*, Lady Amabel? Oh, shame!"

"Don't throw yourself into such a pucker! I did not mean to embark upon a gay round of dissipation." Mab suspected it was as much the result of her Cousin Henrietta's appearance as of her spouse's disappearance that Nell was looking so pulled-about. "There are a great many more worthwhile things to do with one's time than to sit around and *brood*."

With this viewpoint—brooding being one of her own favorite occupations—Henrietta naturally did not agree. Before she could speak, Eleanor did so. "What had you in mind, Mab?" said she.

Mab was pleased to see Nell rouse; putting off the inquisitive Henrietta was very uphill work. "I thought we might explore the house," she responded with a meaningful glance.

Lady March did not take note of her friend's speaking expression, being engrossed in the bone designs of fruit and birds and flowers which adorned her bedpost, as well as in her own unhappy thoughts. "Why should I wish to explore my own house?" she inquired plaintively. "I *live* here."

This was an awkward business! Lady Amabel charitably decided that prolonged exposure to a lugubrious curmudgeon like Henrietta must blunt the usual keenness of anyone's response. "Not in the attics!" she responded, and in case her point was not taken gave Eleanor a sharp pinch. "I'll wager there must be all manner of treasures hidden away."

"Treasure?" In addition to her other little flaws of character, Henrietta was not free of avarice.

"Treasure indeed!" If belatedly aroused, Nell's perceptions were acute. "Broken furniture and outdated clothing, not to mention mice. It is very dreary stuff, Mab. Still, if it will please you—"

28

"Oh, yes!" Mab peered cautiously through the bed-hangings and was very satisfied with Henrietta's look of distaste. "I don't mind mice; we're used to them at the Hall. They don't make a nuisance of themselves if you have a broom and don't mind the mess attendant upon squishing them. We will need to have a broom along with us anyway, because I daresay the attics are full of dust and cobwebs. Do not look so unhappy, Nell! I will defend you! It is not often that the creatures will *attack*—though I do recall an instance when one of our dairymaids had a mouse run up her skirts—" Mab had the satisfaction of seeing Henrietta abruptly depart the room. "Silly widgeon!" she remarked, though did not explain whether this unflattering judgment applied to Henrietta or to the unfortunate dairy maid. "Now we are private at last, Nell. What a dreadful creature Henrietta is! I wonder you have not asked her to leave the house."

"Would that I might!" Lady March leaned back among her pillows and heaved a great sigh. "Henrietta is such a prodigious bore that one feels sorry for her, somehow—although I may yet lose my temper if I must listen to much more drivel about being trained in a school of sorrow, and resignation and consolation and the will of God! You must not antagonize her, Mab. Henrietta is very likely to write to your father, if she suspects he doesn't know you are here." Irritably, she pushed at the wide lace of her nightcap, the better to view her young friend. "He must be very worried about you, Mab."

"I doubt he has even noticed that I am missing." Mab's pretty face was wry. "You know what Papa is! Do not be imagining that he will be as distrait as you were over Marriot. *If* he notices I am not there, he will simply assume he has forgotten where I've gone. But to please you, Nell, I will send him a note. I will remind him you wrote and asked me to come and share your vigil. Papa can't take exception to *that*, because he is always saying I must learn to be kind to those who are less fortunate than I! And you *are* less fortunate, dear

Nell, because I don't have to hide Fergus in the attics!" She laid a thoughtful finger alongside her nose. "Perhaps Fergus may be able to help us straighten out this coil."

Lady March knew her young friend too well to be surprised by this intimation that she was destined to become closely acquainted with the gentleman whom Mab's father had stigmatized as a popinjay. "I will admit I *have* been dull as ditchwater," she allowed.

"I shall tell Papa that I consider it my duty to animate your spirits," mused Mab and then smiled. "Which you can't deny I already *have!* Since my arrival things have gotten positively *lively*. The cook, incidentally, is very wroth this morning, because it appears one of the servants raided the larder in the middle of the night. We need not worry that Marriot shall starve, at any rate!" Curiously she observed her companion, whose shadowed eyes hinted at insufficient sleep. Precisely what had troubled Nell's slumbers, Mab sought to discreetly discover. "Did Marriot, ah, change his mind about—"

"I know what about!" snapped Eleanor. "No, he did not!"

"Then *that* is why you are feeling so very cross!" Lady Amabel gave her friend's hand a sympathetic little pat. "Sometimes the gentlemen can be such perfect gudgeons, with their silly notions of what is honorable and what is not. Still, in this instance, Marriot *does* have a point. I daresay that under the circumstances it would be easier on you, were you to have to see him hanged—*not* that I expect things to come to that!" Her piquant face turned pensive. "*How* much Marriot must love you, to act in *such* a way! Fergus would not be half so self-sacrificing. I vow I am quite envious of you."

What in her present situation anyone could find to envy, Lady March could not decide, being in no mood to appreciate her husband's nobility of character. Another matter concerned her more deeply at this moment. "*Hanged?*" she echoed.

Lady Amabel's tender heart was wrung by her

30

friend's horrified expression; apparently Nell did not altogether realize the implications of their fix. Would anything be served by an avoidance of the truth? Mab decided it would not. Perhaps awareness of the perils of the situation might assist Lord and Lady March to concentrate their minds.

"I do not like to be the one to tell you this!" Amabel said sadly. "Though I am not *altogether* certain, Nell, I think jewel thieves are always hanged."

CHAPTER FOUR

With footsteps hastened by a persistent vision of her husband dangling from the gallows, Lady March made her way to the attics. She had not exaggerated when she told her friend Amabel about the more unusual amenities of the house. The secret room in the attics had been contrived by an earlier Lord March who, in the course of a stormy political career, had incurred the displeasure of both Charles II and Cromwell. Entry was through a secret door, which to the uninformed eye merely appeared as a triangular flap of plaster framed in wood between three beams.

Though not commodious, the hidden room was comfortable enough. Light entered through a small window cunningly placed so as to be visible from neither ground nor roof. Because the room backed onto one of the house's main chimneys, it was tolerably warm. Old carpeting lay thick upon the floor, to muffle footsteps and sound. Lord March himself lay stretched out, snoozing, beneath the old fur cloak on his narrow bed. On the floor beside him an empty tray bore mute evidence as to who had raided the larder. Lady March stood gazing somberly down upon her spouse. "Oh, Marriot!" she whispered, softly. "Hanged!"

"Nell!" Lord March was instantly alert. He swung his long legs over the side of the bed and reached to light a candle that stood on a small chest beside an old Toledo walking sword. This chest, the bed, and two simple stools comprised the chamber's furnishings. The only other luxuries were the painted cloths—featuring such classical subjects as Venus pursuing Adonis—which hung upon the walls. "*Who* was hanged?"

Sadly, Lady March looked upon her husband, who was looking nigh-irresistible, his green eyes laughing up at her, his dark hair tousled from sleep. "No one—yet," she said ominously, as he helped relieve her of her burdens, which included a basin of warm water and a cloth with which to bathe his wound. "Mab assures me that thieves invariably meet that unhappy fate. Not that I believe *you* are a thief, Marriot! But I fear someone who did not know you as well as I would not feel so certain of your innocence."

Lord March himself was not altogether convinced that his honor was so pristine. "It is the very devil of a coil," he responded, wincing as Nell pressed the damp cloth to his head. "Gently, puss! I have lain awake half the night trying to remember what I've been doing and where I've been—to no avail. It is the queerest sensation, to find that all memory of a portion of your life has flown straight out of your mind."

Lady March, too, had enjoyed fitful slumber, her rest disturbed by a persistent recurrent image of her spouse clad in naught but stolen jewels. "We assume they are stolen, but perhaps they are not. Perhaps you came by them in some unexceptionable way."

"Unexceptionable?" Lord March turned and caught his wife's ministering hand and pulled her down to sit beside him on the bunk. He dragged forward the valise. "Certainly I would like to think so—but we must be reasonable, puss!"

Gloomily, Lady March stared at the valise's contents. It was most unlikely that such a large quantity of jewels could be claimed by any one person. "Perhaps you meant to make me a present," she suggested without much hope.

"A present, Nell?" Marriot held up a chain of heavy gold set with huge pearls interspersed with rubies. "I would hardly consider this in your style! And though my memory has played me false of late, I have forgot nothing *before* I left White's that fateful night—including the fact that you aren't fond of jewels." He dropped the chain back into the valise and shoved it aside. "As for me dancing the Paddington frisk, don't

33

think it! We're not done for yet. I'll have a word to say to young Mab about giving you such a fright."

"You must not scold Mab, Marriot; she promises to be the most resourceful of allies." As her husband sought to repair the worst of the ravages wrought to his person by his adventures, Lady March wrapped herself in the fur cloak. "Even now she diverts Cousin Henrietta so that *my* disappearance will not be remarked. I left them talking about the preparations our countrymen have taken against the threatened French invasion. Mab was trying to persuade Henrietta to join the militia, I think."

Lord March stripped off his shirt. "I wish her joy of the task."

Wistfully, Lady March eyed her husband's bare, bronzed torso, its excellent muscular development shown to good advantage by the flickering candlelight. "It was *you* who turned me absolutely sick with fright! Can you not imagine my horror when you failed to come home?"

Marriot paused in his ablutions, which he was performing with the only means at hand, the water with which his wife had bathed his head. How delectable she looked curled up on his bed, the fur cloak clutched around her, chestnut curls coming loose. He had a sudden impulse to bury his fingers in that heavy hair, to press his lips against her throat, to fling aside the cloak—How intently her amber eyes fixed on his face, how lovely was the flush on her cheeks, how inviting her crooked smile. Hastily Lord March donned the fresh shirt which she'd brought. Eleanor sighed.

"I am truly sorry for the anxiety I have caused you," said Marriot, taking up a stance at a prudent distance from the bed. "I am even sorrier that it seems I am destined to cause you still more. The longer I ponder my possession of those accursed jewels, the more questionable that possession seems. In short, I am very much afraid that I have been up to no good."

Lady March was in this moment a great deal less concerned with her husband's fears than with her own

34

rapid pulse. "I don't care a button *what* you have been up to," she said crossly. "I wish you would cease acting so *missish,* Marriot! The very least you might do after causing me so much anguish is kiss me—even if your scruples forbid you doing else. We are supposed to be secret, remember. We will not long continue so if we must converse at a shout."

This latter argument—the last person whom he wanted involved in his dilemma was his Cousin Henrietta—brought Lord March back to the narrow bed. "Vixen!" he said, and awarded his wife a chaste salute. Lady March, however, possessed not a single scruple, at least in regard to her racing pulse, and the caress which she in turn pressed upon her husband had nothing in it that was chaste. Some time elasped in this manner, while Lord and Lady March struggled with his lordship's conscience. Eventually, and reluctantly, Marriot won. Gently, he disengaged himself. "Try and understand. I cannot come to you with a stain upon my honor, Nell."

Neither did Lady March care a button for this inconvenient selflessness. "You don't need to come to me! We are already married!" she tearfully pointed out. "And it is very bad of you to be so *distant* when at any moment you may be hanged as a thief!"

Though Lord March was hard pressed to keep to his good intentions—with such sweet abandon did his wife weep upon his chest—the thought of his own imminent execution was a great help. "I trust it will not come to that," he soothed, as he wiped the moisture from her cheeks. "You must be very brave, puss, and help me to establish my innocence. We cannot expect the authorities to believe that I have no notion of how I came by these jewels. The best thing I can do is keep dubber-mum'd for the nonce."

"'Dubber-mum'd'?" Lady March allowed herself one last sniffle. "What is *that?*"

"Be quiet." Lord March dropped a caress upon the tip of his wife's nose. "That is, 'dubber-mum'd' *means* to keep a still tongue in one's head." He frowned. "I wonder how I came by that queer phrase. There are more: to snack the bit means to share the money; hub and grub are food and drink—I fear, my darling, that the company I have been keeping is not *quite* the thing!"

"You must try even harder to remember." As if to aid her husband in this enterprise, Lady March rubbed her nose against his lean cheek. "That is the only way we may make sense of this. No matter how little you may think of yourself, *I* know you have done nothing so dreadfully bad. Oh, *why* must you remain hidden away like—like some common thief?"

All that Lord March could think about while holding his adored wife so close in his arms had little to do with his mysterious forgotten past. Abruptly, he abandoned the bed and perched instead upon the chest. "I do not care to see my family plunged into some vile scandal," he retorted. "Do not argue with me, Nell! My mind is quite made up on that point. My return must not be made public until some reasonable explanation of my absence has been devised."

Though Lady March was not all disposed to keep her distance, she temporarily acquiesced to her husband's obvious intention of keeping her at arm's length. Clearly, the quickest resolution to this absurd dilemma was to solve the perplexing problem of the stolen gems. "But no one even knows you *have* them!" Eleanor pointed out.

This happy notion had also occurred to Marriot. "We don't *know* that. And we dare not assume it, I fear. Much as I would like to tuck the things away somewhere and forget their existence, I cannot do so. For my transgressions—whatever they may be!—I would not have *you* stand the consequence." His mobile face was wry. "Poor puss! You will wish you were not so eager to have me come home."

"Bosh!" In lieu of a husbandly embrace, Nell burrowed closer into the fur cloak, a meager substitute. "It would take more than a little inconvenience to make me suffer a revulsion of feeling, Marriot. If only Cousin Henrietta were not here, so that we would not have to be put to these abominable expedients and shifts! I dare not send her away *now,* lest her suspicions are aroused—*you* know how she is! Let her get a notion that something is in the wind and she will be forever breathing down my neck."

Lord March's green eyes rested somewhat wistfully upon his wife's neck, which was encircled by the ruff of her high-waisted white cambric gown. Lady March caught his glance. Equally wistful, she continued, "I am not good at dissembling, but I shall try very hard! Perhaps Henrietta may attribute any oddity to the anguish I suffer as result of our separation—oh, Marriot! Truly I am full of admiration for your nobility of character, and I think it is very *good* of you to try and spare my feelings, even though it makes me melancholy, and I would much rather you would *not.* Because I do not *care* if you stole those wretched jewels!"

So moved was Lord March by this highly biased outburst that he arose from the chest to pace in very great affliction up and down the room. "A pretty companion that would make me!" he said bitterly. "I cannot think a criminal would be the proper husband for you, Nell."

"A criminal? Pooh!" Not only did the fur cloak lack the ability to comfort, it had grown stifling hot. "You refine too much upon it."

"No, I do not." With amusement, Lord March watched his wife struggle to be free of the cloak. After a moment, he crossed to her and plucked it away. How very desirable she looked curled up on his bed, watching him through those clear, cool amber eyes. "I have given every appearance of being a very loose fish. Yes, I know you cannot enter into my feelings upon that head, but I beg you will oblige me in it all the same—tiresome creature though you may think me."

"I do not think you are tiresome! No, nor a loose fish!" Anxious that her husband be rid of these apprehensions, Lady March flung herself upon his chest, grasped his arms, and gazed anxiously up into his face. "You have overlooked the most pertinent point of all. I *love* you, Marriot."

Green eyes met amber, and held. "And I," Lord March said huskily, "love you, Nell!"

No little time later, Lord and Lady March were snuggled very comfortably beneath the fur cloak upon the narrow little bed. "I should be very angry with you," remarked his lordship to his wife. "I *had* meant to deal with you from a discreet distance—don't poker up on me, puss! I like it excessively that you have persuaded me I should not! Unfortunately, this does not alter the situation, about which we have not yet decided what to do."

"What *can* we do?" Now that she was no longer plagued by racing pulses, Lady March could approach the problem with a much clearer mind. To further speed her thought processes, she leaned across her husband's chest, propped her elbows on either side of him, and gazed dreamily down into his face. "First, I suppose, we must find out if a large amount of jewelry has been stolen recently. I do not like to ask Cousin Henrietta lest she grow suspicious. I think Mab and I must develop a passion for the newssheets."

"I do not like to involve you in this business." Lord March indulged his impulse to bury his hands in his wife's thick hair. "I will undertake my own inquiries."

"No!" Pleasant as it was to be caressed, Lady March abruptly drew back. "You must not!"

In lieu of her hair, Marriot stroked Eleanor's bare shoulder. "Whyever not, puss? I will be very careful and leave by the old tunnel after the household is asleep."

How best to explain this conviction that disaster would befall them were Marriot to step foot outside Marcham Towers? Frantically, Nell thought. "If you did *not* steal the jewels, then how came you to have them? Even now someone may be looking for you—if not the jewels' owners, then the thieves responsible for their disappearance. I'll warrant you have not thought of *that!*" Her eyes filled with tears. *"Pray* oblige me in this, Marriot! Let Mab and me see what we may discover. To lose you again, so soon after having you restored to me, would be more than flesh and blood can tolerate!"

Appalled that he had inadvertently distressed his wife, Lord March rained kisses on her shoulder, neck and cheek. "Don't go into high fidgets!" he soothed. "We will try it your way. You and Mab discover what you can. Meantime I will strive my utmost to avoid Cousin Henrietta. Don't fret, Nell! Marcham Towers is large enough to safely hide several fugitives, especially one who knows its nooks and crannies like the palm of his own hand." If not better, he silently amended, having already discovered that appendage to be inexplicably callused.

Eleanor, too, had noted those new calluses, about which she breathed not a word. So relieved was Nell to have Marriot restored that she cared not a fig if he had *murdered* someone. In point of fact, Nell had several times experienced an urge to commit murder herself.

Briskly, she set aside all thought of Cousin Henrietta, refusing to further tarnish this golden hour. "I brought you some things to make you more comfortable," she said to Marriot.

His smile was frankly appreciative. "So you did."

Nell blushed and giggled, "Rogue! I meant that I had brought another candle, and some fruit, and some books so that you may not be bored. Very highly, I recommend *The History of Serpents*—did you know dragons get fat on eggs? I assure you it is true. The adult dragon swallows eggs whole, then rolls about 'til the shells are crushed inside him. And in case you do not care for dragons, I have brought you Pliny's *Natural History*, and Foxe's *Book of Martyrs*, and several more."

Now it was Lord March who propped himself up on an elbow. With lazy amusement he watched his wife struggle to fasten herself in her high-waisted dress—rumpled now, and damp from the water basin, and none improved by a close acquaintance with cobwebs and dust. "When will you return?" he inquired.

"As soon as I may—or perhaps I will send Mab!"

Lady March smoothed ineffectively at her tumbled locks. "*What* a sight I must look. It is not kind in you to laugh at me, you wretch!" Her own smile faded. "Marriot, there is something we must consider. I do not think you stole the jewels, of course—but if we cannot prove it, then what?"

No trace of amusement remained on Lord March's features as he reached over the side of the bed and plucked his shirt from off the floor. "There is another possibility, though you will not care to consider it. Perhaps I *am* guilty of theft—in which case I shall take my punishment like a man. My darling, do not look *so!* I doubt myself that will turn out to be the case."

"No, no, I do not think it!" Nell pressed cold fingers to her cheeks. "I have just remembered the most appalling thing. Marriot, when days passed and you did not come home—I would not do it *now*, but then I had no notion—oh, *blast!* I called in Bow Street!"

CHAPTER FIVE

Fergus Ridpath, Baron Parrington, gazed without noticeable enthusiasm upon Marcham Towers. For the record, let it be stated that few people, especially of the feminine persuasion, could gaze with a similar lack of enthusiasm upon Lord Parrington. At seven-and-twenty Fergus had golden hair and brown eyes set in an amazingly handsome countenance, nicely fashioned shoulders and calves and all else in between. This day he wore a topcoat of light tan broadcloth with collar of gold velvet, a high-crowned beaver hat, gloves of York tan, buckskin breeches, and tall boots with tassels and white tops. "This *is* Lady Amabel's direction," he said reassuringly to his companion. "Allow me to assist you to mount the steps, Mama."

Bedazzling as was Lord Parrington to behold, similar approbation did not apply to his sole surviving parent. Lady Katherine's figure was stooped, her countenance raddled; once a great beauty, she now appeared older than her actual years. Nor was her personality any more pleasing than her person. "Lady Amabel!" she muttered irritably, as she contrived to mount the steps with the combined assistance of son and silver-headed cane. "Plague take the chit!"

Lord Parrington's admirers were prone to wax eloquent about his unflagging patience regarding his vituperative parent. "I know you do not mean that, Mama!" he said cheerfully. "You are merely cross because you do not like to travel. I warned you of how it would be, but you were determined to accompany me to town. I did not realize you were so taken with Lady Amabel. She will be prodigious pleased by so high a mark of favor."

"Taken with her, am I?" One of the disadvantages

attached to unflagging good humor and an upright un-subtle nature was the tendency to attribute to other people the sterling qualities possessed by oneself. Lady Katherine did indeed wish Amabel might be carried off by plague. Her usually docile son had inexplicably taken the notion that he must set up his nursery, and for his purpose had settled upon the loveliest girl in the neighborhood, unfortunately the daughter of a lowly baronet. "*Taken* with her? Egad!"

Lord Parrington made no response to this cryptic remark, being busy anticipating Lady Amabel's reaction to the singular stroke of good fortune which was about to befall her in the person of himself. Fergus was not vain, precisely, but he had been brought up to have an excellent notion of his own worth. His mother doted on him, and Fergus expected other ladies to similarly react. Thus far, though his experience had been some-what limited, he'd had no cause for disappointment. Complacently, Lord Parrington smoothed the sleeve of his broadcloth topcoat.

While the baron and his mama had thus engaged in rumination, the ancient door had opened to them, and they had been admitted into the great hall. There they were left to inspect the suits of armor and racks of spears, the screen of carved and wainscoted wood that stood at one end of the chamber. More precisely, Lord Parrington inspected those antiquities. Lady Katherine took firm grasp upon her cane and glowered at the staircase. At length the servant reappeared and con-ducted them past the carved balustrades and newel posts picked out in bright colors, and into the solar.

Not Lady Amabel awaited there, as Fergus had an-ticipated, but a short, plump, agitated-looking lady with wispy white hair. "I am so sorry!" gasped this worthy as she hastened to greet them, an act accom-panied by a great fluttering of her hands. "Amabel will wish she had been here to welcome you—so kind of you to call! So condescending! It is the fault of this queer old house that she is *not* with us at the moment; things—and people!—are never where one expects them to be. But I am forgetting to introduce myself! Henrietta Dougharty—March's cousin, you know!"

"March?" Lady Katherine settled stiffly upon the chocolate-red daybed, her hands resting before her on the knob of her cane. "Dougharty? I seem to know that name. Are your people from Suffolk?"

Looking very gratified, Henrietta perched primly on a nearby embroidered chair. "Why, yes!" she replied. Lord Parrington left the ladies to the exploration of respective genealogies. As result of Mab's failure to greet him in a properly flattered manner, he was becoming somewhat miffed. Mab could not have been *certain* he would come to London as result of her cryptic summons. The gist of that letter, Fergus pondered once more. He could make no sense of the strange goings-on at which Mab had hinted. She had called her papa the greatest wretch in nature, Fergus reflected. Mab was a great deal *less* charitable toward her parent than the young man he'd called a popinjay.

"Fergus! Pay attention!" his own peevish parent snapped. "Dougharty and I have discovered we are old acquaintances. Tell me, ma'am, how is it that Lady Amabel came to you? An unexpected visit, was it not?"

Henrietta was gratified beyond measure by this familiar treatment—Lady Katherine might have married a mere baron, but she was a duke's daughter, a fact none of her acquaintance were permitted to forget. *"Quite* unexpected!" agreed Henrietta, her expression arch. "It was not *me* she came to, precisely, but Eleanor—that is, Lady March. *How* I wish I knew where they have got to! The attics, perhaps."

"Attics?" Lady Katherine began to wonder if this relic of her childhood—it had been established that the ladies had been girls together in Suffolk—had grown queer in the head. "Plague on't, why the *attics?* I do not scruple to tell you, Dougharty, that this is an exceedingly ill-run house. And inconvenient." She gazed disapprovingly about her. "It is a veritable antique."

"It is also very cold." Henrietta pulled her square Scotch shawl of silk and cotton around her shoulders, which were somewhat prematurely swathed in black bombazine. "The attics were Lady Amabel's suggestion. I believe she wished to explore them. There was some talk of forgotten treasures." She shuddered. "And mice!"

Though Lady Katherine was too starched up to shudder, she fumbled for her vinaigrette. "Mice!" she repeated, astonished. "What does the chit want with *mice?*"

Henrietta struggled with the temptation to unburden herself to this sympathetic listener, and lost. "She *said* she wished to smash them with a broom! I daresay she didn't mean it, any more than she meant it when she suggested we ladies should join the militia, and arm ourselves with spades and axes, and prepare to see that the beacons are properly lit."

Upon receipt of this startling intelligence, Lady Katherine cast her son a pointed glance. Occupied with a vision of Lady Amabel advancing upon one of the many circular martello towers which had recently sprung up about the countryside, Fergus did not notice his mama's look. Mab would have her skirts pinned up, he mused, thus displaying her pretty ankles, and would defend herself with a pitchfork. Though in reality he would never condone such an improper action, it made an amusing thought. He then fell into pleasant contemplation of Lady Amabel's ankles, which he had never seen.

"Stab me!" muttered Lady Katherine, growing steadily more out of charity with her son.

"So you may say." Henrietta leaned closer, increasingly drawn to this lady who was obviously no admirer of the irrepressible Mab. "It is my impression that Lady Amabel's arrival had something very *odd* about it. I know Eleanor did not expect her, else I would have been *told*. Furthermore, unless I am very much mistaken, and I do not see how I *could* be, she arrived in the middle of the night!"

Though Henrietta might be shivering in the chill air of the solar—Fergus having unwittingly stolen a leaf from her own book in his inspection of the fireplace, and now blocking all the heat—Lady Katherine was considerably warmer. Not only was Lord Parrington's mama dressed to withstand the most inclement of weather, muffled up in twilled worsted; a tippet with long hanging ends wrapped around her neck, and a bonnet of gros de Naples with ribbon ties concealing her hair and ears and a portion of her face; but she also experienced the heady flush of a hunter whose quarry has abruptly come into sight. That Lady Katherine did not intend her son to marry anyone, and thus rend the delicate fabric of her own very comfortable existence, perhaps need not be explained.

"I have harbored doubts about Lady Amabel for some time," she whispered, leaning so far forward that she almost touched the knob of her walking stick with her chin. "One does not like to cast aspersions, but I have seen no indication that the chit has the slightest sense of what is and isn't nice. I will be frank, Dougharty! You at least I know will feel just as you should! I was actually *glad* to hear that the chit had come to London, for she had set her cap at my son."

"Oh, I say!" Henrietta stared at the Exquisite, currently studying through his quizzing glass Diana bathing upon the chimney piece. "I feel for you, Lady Katherine—indeed I do. I have long held that Amabel is incorrigible! She possesses what I fear is an incurable levity—but I must not speak unfavorably of a guest in this house."

Disappointed, because she wished very much to hear further adverse comments on this topic, Lady Katherine sat once more erect. "We were very nicely placed in the country, before Fergus took the notion that he must come to London," she sighed. "I could not dissuade him, though ordinarily he is a good obedient boy, and very considerate, and a great solace to me." She looked arch. "Fergus could serve as a model of good breeding for any amount of romantical misses, I vow! Certainly any number of misses have wished that he might.

Though I should not say so, Dougharty, my son is a bachelor of the first stare."

Lord Parrington would remain a bachelor, thought Henrietta, had Lady Katherine her way. Henrietta saw nothing to censure in this ambition which, had she possessed a son, she would doubtless have shared. In fact, Henrietta wished Lady Katherine every success in detaching her son from Amabel, to whom by prolonged exposure Henrietta had not grown endeared.

Impatient for agreement, Lady Katherine poked Henrietta with her cane. Henrietta stared. "I *said*," repeated Lady Katherine, "that my son is a bachelor of the first stare."

"Indeed!" Henrietta blanched, aware she'd caused offense. "A gentleman of position and substance—well-connected—any young woman must count herself fortunate!"

Lady Katherine was not pleased by this restriction; in her opinion, no female young *or* old could be insensible to her offspring's good looks and charm. She did not quibble, lest her displeasure reduce her new-found ally to incoherence. Though Lady Katherine ordinarily derived considerable satisfaction from causing lesser beings to quiver like blancmange, no further adverse intelligence concerning Amabel could thereby be learned.

"*Most* young women would realize their good fortune," she remarked, surveying the solar with unabated distaste. "From Lady Amabel's absence, we must assume that she does *not*. I *had* hoped Fergus would not be disappointed in the chit, but my hopes are unfulfilled, alas. Now perhaps he may be persuaded to go home! This racketing about the countryside is no treat for a woman of my age—or enfeebled health." Recalled to her weak condition, Lady Katherine partook of her vinaigrette. "It is a mother's duty to sacrifice herself! Fergus has not the least notion of how to go on, the lamb."

Well did Henrietta know the discomforts of travel, due to her own frequent journeys from relative to relative, undertaken not only in search of scandal but also to escape the tedium of her own shabby little house. Sympathetically, she regarded her companion.

"Who is a lamb?" inquired Lord Parrington, having tired of Diana bathing amid monkeys and birds and beasts upon the fireplace. Secretly, he had also grown weary with waiting for Amabel to grace the solar with her presence. Though Fergus was far from the popinjay Mab's father considered him—there was nothing of the fop in him—he was very correct. No son of Lady Katherine's could fail to be so. Relentlessly coached in deportment by his mama, Fergus had all his life trod the road of dignity and decorum. One of the things which attracted him to Lady Amabel was her refreshing spontaneity. Between Mab's mysteriously urgent note and subsequent failure to appear, however, he was beginning to feel ill-used.

"*You* are a lamb, my son!" Doting looks sat ill upon Lady Katherine's raddled face. "We will take our leave now, Dougharty. You may tell Lady Amabel we called to see her. A pity the chit didn't see fit to spare a moment of her precious time. But that is the way with these young girls. In *our* day we were better brought up!"

Though a trifle out of charity with the subject of this tirade, Lord Parrington was not so quick to censure as his parent. "You are merely tired, Mama!" he soothed, and assisted her to rise. "Else you would realize there is doubtless some good reason for Lady Amabel's absence, and would not be so out-of-reason cross."

Devoted as she was to her sole offspring, Lady Katherine sometimes found his tendency to see the best in everyone extremely annoying. Since this was one of those times, she irritably shook off his helping hand. "I'd like to know what that reason might be!" she snapped.

"Can it be you do not know?" Henrietta was mislead into crediting not Lady Katherine's true sentiment, but her words. "About Marriot?" It was clear from the callers' blank expressions that they were not aware of the bizarre disappearance of Lord March. Eagerly, Henrietta explained, concluding, "Whether it was a press gang that took him, or French agents, or tinkers, no one can say! We are in anxious expectation of more news—although I expect that when the news *does* come, it will be much too dreadful to bear!" She pressed her hands to her bombazine-swathed bosom. "Poor, poor Nell!"

"Faith, I've never heard of such a thing." Disapproval was writ large on Lady Katherine's ruined face. The inexplicable disappearance of a peer she could not help but consider ill-bred.

This aspect of the situation did not present itself to Fergus, who had exchanged his vision of Mab lighting beacons for one of that damsel tending selflessly to Lady March, understandably disconsolate and prostrate. He had not previously realized this generous side to Mab's nature. Of course he must forgive her for not putting in an appearance in the solar when her reasons were so pure. "What a *good* girl she is!" he said.

A good girl? Lady Katherine had no doubt for whom this sobriquet was intended. She took firmer grasp on her cane. "Nothing of this sort has ever happened in *our* family!" she somewhat unnecessarily pointed out. "Doubtless the explanation will turn out to have to do with a woman. When gentlemen make jack-puddings of themselves, some female is generally involved." The look she bestowed upon her son clearly indicated the opinion that he was threatened by this ignominious fate.

"Pray give Lady Amabel our regards," murmured Lord Parrington, oblivious to his mama's malice, bending in a courtly manner over Henrietta's hand. "And tell her that I shall engage myself to call upon her again tomorrow."

"*Not* tomorrow; *I* shall require your services!" To underscore her point, and relieve her burgeoning displeasure, Lady Katherine prodded her son with her cane. Far too well-bred to take exception to this treatment, Lord Parrington smiled ruefully. "If not tomorrow," he told Henrietta, "then *soon!*"

CHAPTER SIX

Though Lady Amabel's reasons for not greeting her callers in the solar were not what Lord Parrington imagined, they were still very sound: first, Mab didn't realize that she *had* visitors; and second, she was engaged during that portentous interlude in playing at whist with Lord March. So far as the cards were concerned, as had rapidly become apparent, Lady Amabel's luck was out.

"You will be wondering why I have run away from home!" she said, throwing down her cards. "It is because Papa is so stubborn—well, *you* know what he is! Or do you? It is very queer how you recall some things, and others you do not."

"Not so queer as all that." Lord March pushed aside the abandoned cards and stretched out his long legs on the bed. "I remember everything up to the point when I 'disappeared' on my way home from White's. Only then does memory fail. It is my theory I *was* attacked by footpads, and struck, and lost all notion of who I was until the other night when I was again assaulted." His expression was wry. "You look skeptical, brat! I cannot blame you for doubting so farfetched a tale. But if you are doubtful, others will be even more so, I think."

"Doubtless you are correct." Mab drew her cloak closer about her and settled more comfortably upon the wooden chest. "Let us test your theory! How much are you aware of what has happened, during your absence, in the world? Do you know, for instance, that Bonaparte spent the summer drilling his *Grande Armée*? They marched about in rhythm with songs about sailing for England. Now he has crowned himself Emperor. It's said he paid the husband of an actress thousands of francs to stage-manage the ceremony."

"And at the last moment Mme. Bonaparte confessed to the Pope that she was no more than a legalized concubine, and a hasty religious marriage took place. There were conflicting versions—clever Josephine trapped the Emperor, or the Emperor trapped the Pope, or the Pope stood his ground and made them both look absurd." In his turn, Lord March looked ruminative. "It would seem I can remember *some* things."

"Mayhap the rest will come back to you." Lady Amabel wrinkled her pretty nose. "Perhaps if *I* were to hit you on the head—"

"Pernicious wench!" responded Lord March, amused. "Since whist is too dull for you, shall we play a rubber or two of piquet?" Mab immediately agreed. A brief silence descended upon the secret room.

"Blast!" muttered Mab, a reckless player. Hoping for a change each rubber, she had risked all on the chance of a maddeningly elusive coup. "I think that during your absence you must have been an ivory tuner, or a Captain Sharp! A gentleman should not trounce a lady shamelessly at cards, but at least let her *think* she may win."

"A lady, perhaps." Lord March grinned. "But not a little baggage whom he once dandled on his knee."

"Did you really?" Mab's imagination was caught by this suggestion. A gentleman fond enough to bounce her upon his knee might well be persuaded to intercede on her behalf with her misguided papa.

"I did." Marriot's long acquaintance with Lady Amabel had taught him to recognize and distrust the speculative gleam currently present in her blue eyes. Loweringly, he added, "And very damp you were! No, my girl, you will not pitchfork *me* into this battle of wills you are having with your papa. I have difficulties of my own to resolve, in case you have forgot."

A good-hearted girl, Lady Amabel could not argue this point; and even had she been inclined to, there was not sufficient time. With a faint groan of protest, the secret panel swung slowly open. Mab leapt to her feet, clutching the ancient Toledo sword.

"What the *devil?*" inquired Lady March somewhat faintly, due to the sharp blade pointed at her throat.

"How was I to know it was only you?" responded Amabel, lowering the sword. "I thought perhaps Henrietta had discovered the entrance."

"Even if she *does* discover it, I do not think we can permit you to cut her throat, infant." Lord March's tone was preoccupied, his attention all for his wife. Eleanor was dressed for the out-of-doors in a long black redingote with high collar and sleeves, a straw hat turned up in front and trimmed with green ribbons, half boots of kid, buff-colored suede gloves, and huge bearskin muff. "You're cold, Nell! Come here and sit beside me and let me make you warm." Lord March made room for her beside him on the bed.

"Marriot!" Eleanor sighed, blushing, and complied.

Lady Amabel sighed also, not only from envy, but also because she foresaw that Lord and Lady March were again on the verge of abandoning practical matters in favor of romance. "I wish the pair of you might try for a little common sense!" she scolded. "To cuddle *now* is like Nero fiddling while Rome burned. It *was* Nero who did so, was it not? No matter! Nell, what did you find out?"

"Hmm? Ah!" With difficulty, Lady March detached her gaze from her husband's face. "I am being very foolish, I know, but I have been in such a whirl. Lest she demand to accompany me, I dared not let Henrietta discover I planned to leave the house. To do so without her knowledge was no easy feat! She did not remark my return, fortunately. She was entertaining someone in the solar, so I simply slipped by."

"Entertaining?" Lady Amabel's lively curiosity was aroused. "Who?"

"Had I paused to discover *that,* I would have never escaped." Looking both irritable and tragic, Eleanor reached into her huge muff and withdrew a bottle of claret. "You're going to need this, Marriot. We *all* shall, unless I am mistaken about what I heard in the streets."

51

"In the streets?" echoed Lord March, glancing in some perplexity from the claret bottle to his wife's mournful face. Even in the grip of a fit of the blue devils she was nigh-irresistible. "My darling!" he murmured, touching tender fingers to her face. "*My* darling!" responded Eleanor, passionately kissing his hands. "I will not let you be hanged!"

"Hanged? Piffle!" Impatient of these ill-timed declarations, Mab reached for the folded newssheet which had also been hidden in Nell's muff. "I admit that Marriot's case does not look especially promising, but we shall make a recover—the deuce!"

This exclamation, uttered in shocked tones, temporarily roused Lord and Lady March from preoccupation with themselves. Both turned to Mab. Wide-eyed, that young lady was avidly scanning the newssheet. "A parure of rubies and emeralds!" she read aloud when made aware of their attention. "A brooch composed of a spray of diamond flowers set in silver leaves! A heavy golden chain set with one hundred and sixty pearls, every sixteen divided by a large ruby—the latest in a series of appalling, brutal robberies that has for several months plagued the metropolis—the most unstinting inquiries are being made! Marriot!"

Lady March, whose nerves were not surprisingly shattered, found in this unsympathetic pronouncement cause for grave offense. "*How* can you think—as if Marriot *could*—and after I took you in without a word of the scolding you deserved—"

"Come, Nell, do not take on so!" interrupted Marriot, and drew his wife into his arms. With a last incoherent utterance, which sounded amazingly like "ungrateful little twit," Nell subsided upon his chest.

Philosophically, Mab accepted her friend's censure, though from any other source it would have prompted her to cut up very stiff. "We are agreed that Marriot is incapable of so abominable a proceeding," she remarked. "It is my opinion that Marriot interrupted a robbery in progress and was consequently knocked on the head, which caused him to at last remember who

52

he was—and caused him to forget why he was missing all this time." Keenly she regarded Lord March, who had disposed of his wife's inconvenient high-brimmed bonnet so that he might better kiss her brow. "Unless you are playing some deep game, Marriot? I thought not."

Was the absurd child disappointed? Reluctantly Lady March removed herself from her husband's chest. "I should not have fired up at you! I am very sorry for it, Mab. This discovery has utterly sunk my spirits. I had hoped there might be some easy way out of this fix—" In her brown eyes was an anxious expression. "What *do* they do to thieves, exactly? Is anyone certain?"

Though Lord March had not been thrown into a state of consternation so extreme as that which affected his wife, recent events had left him somewhat distressed— so much so that he broached the bottle of claret without a thought for the fact that it had not been benefitted by a severe shaking up. "I do not know precisely," he admitted after taking a deep drink. "I believe that the theft of property worth more than one shilling may be punishable by death."

"One shilling!" Lady March gazed at the shabby valise, the contents of which would have been worth a great deal more than one shilling even had they been made of paste. So disheartening was this realization that Nell plucked the claret bottle out of her husband's hands. "I shall go mad! I am sure of it!" she vowed, and drank.

"Come out of the mops!" said Mab, as in an effort to make herself even more comfortable she tucked her feet—clad in thin pointed shoes without heels—beneath the molting fur cloak. "Naturally you cannot help being alarmed a little by the intelligence that Marriot is in possession of a fortune in stolen gems— but it *is* no more than we had expected! Frankly, Nell, I do not see why you are making such a fuss."

"A fuss!" Lady March looked quite extraordinarily beautiful when animated, or so her husband thought,

53

responding with keen appreciation to her flushed cheeks and sparkling eyes. "So would *you* fuss, Mab, if there was a very real possibility that your—what *is* his name? Fergus!—might be hanged! There is no way we may be rid of the jewels without attracting attention, or none that I can think of—Marriot can hardly walk boldly into Bow Street Public Office, and hand over his valise, and say 'here are your missing baubles, but how I come to have them I have clean forgot'!"

Since she had not been invited to partake of the claret which Lord and Lady March passed back and forth so freely, Mab toyed with the fan. "They *might* believe him," she doubtfully put forth.

"Yes, and they might not." Sadly, Eleanor gazed upon her husband. "I cannot care to take that chance."

"Nor do I." In an attempt to think more clearly, Marriot rose from the narrow bed and began to pace the floor. "Even I must concede that this errant memory makes for a very lame tale. Nor do I care to implicate someone else in my troubles, as would be the case if anyone were to try and give back the gems."

"Perhaps we could say we had just found them?" suggested Amabel, as Eleanor hastily bent to snatch her discarded bonnet out of Marriot's pathway.

"Certainly!" responded Lord March drily. "We could also assure them that pigs may fly!"

Not surprisingly, in view of this uncooperative attitude, conversation lagged. Lord March paced the floor, from his claret bottle taking an occasional absentminded drink; Lady March plucked morosely at the green ribbons of the bonnet she held on her lap. Lady Amabel, meanwhile, sulked behind the bedraggled feathers of her antique fan.

Mab was the first to recover her good humor, perhaps because her own peril was the least. "Then we must discover who the real thieves *are!*" she said.

"Exactly so." Belatedly aware of his selfish usurpation of the claret bottle, Lord March passed it to his wife. "I see nothing for it but that I must undertake inquiries."

"Inquiries? No!" As she leapt up off the bed, Lady March inadvertently crushed her own bonnet underfoot. "What if you run afoul of *real* thieves?"

"And what if Bow Street has got wind *you* have the jewels?" The fan having proved inadequate for her purposes, Mab cooled herself with the newssheet. "I agree you cannot remain hidden here forever, Marriot, but we must not be rash. Your queer disappearance gained a great deal of observation in the world. You are bound to eventually be recognized if you go wandering around the streets."

Lord March roused sufficiently from his preoccupation with his wife, who'd flung herself into his arms, to recognize the force of Mab's arguments. That young lady's fine application of logic did not endear her to him. Marriot had scant liking for this hidden attic room. Though he did not verbalize his dissatisfaction, it was obvious in the choleric glance he awarded the meager furnishings of his chamber, the heavily carpeted floor, the painted cloths hung on the walls. Commented Lady Amabel acutely, "You would be much more uncomfortable in Newgate—or wherever it is they imprison thieves! Truly, I think it is very nice that the two of you dote on one another, and I wish very much that someone might feel similarly toward me— but I feel constrained to point out that if you might *cease* to dote for but a moment, we might discover a way out of this pickle."

Thus abjured, Lord March slowly released his wife, who with an equal lack of enthusiasm removed herself from his chest. Nell sat down on the bed. Marriot propped one foot up beside her. "Well?" he said.

A realistic damsel, Amabel refrained from comment upon the fascination with which Lady March was prone to observe her husband's shapely limb. "I have been thinking how we may most effectively go about solving this puzzle, and I think you must make a reappearance, Marriot."

"No!" wailed Nell, clutching convulsively at her husband's calf. "I beg I may hear no such thing!"

Lord March patted his wife's chestnut locks pressed against his knee. "I fear you must, puss. Try and be my good, brave girl! I am persuaded you would not wish me to remain hidden away here forever, Nell."

On a deep breath, Lady March drew herself erect. "You are right. I am being unforgivably foolish," she said.

"Nonsense! You are a darling!" Marriot caressed Nell's cheek, in return for which he was awarded her irresistibly uneven smile.

Never had Mab seen a more affecting scene. "It is true that Nell and I have little chance of discovering anything of particular import," she inserted, recalling her companions to her presence, and their purpose, before mutual adoration rendered them insensible. "But if you are to undertake your own inquiries, it must not be with the chance of landing in gaol. In short, before you make your reappearance among us, we must devise some unexceptionable tale of where you've been."

CHAPTER SEVEN

Though not habitually an early riser, Lady Amabel had adapted that custom whilst at Marcham Towers; by it she was free to pursue her own inclinations unmolested, while Henrietta remained abed. Inclination this morn had taken Mab to the secret attic room with a breakfast for his lordship and brisk words of encouragement. The breakfast his lordship had appreciated, if not the good advice, in response to which he irritably bade his visitor leave him to his reading, this day a translation of Antonio de Torquenada's *The Spanish Mandeula of Miracles,* which recounted such wonders as the woman who was shipwrecked on an African shore and produced two sons sired by an ape. For his short temper Lady Amabel bore Lord March no grudge. It was no easy thing, this concocting an unexceptionable explanation of a gentleman's prolonged absence from his world. As Mab walked into the solar that matter also occupied her own mind.

That Lady Amabel was rapt in thought was apparent to the young gentleman who awaited there; the better to observe her, he did not immediately speak. As always, Mab was a joy to look upon, this day clad in a pretty high-waisted cotton dress suitable for winter, and a fringed shawl—but did a *cobweb* adorn her dark hair? Was that *dust* upon her skirts? And why was she clutching a very sorry-looking fan? In search of enlightenment, Fergus cleared his throat.

Made aware of the intruder, Mab shrieked and clasped her hands, consequently doing further damage to the ancient fan. Upon realizing the identity of the intruder, she let out her breath. Briefly she allowed herself to contemplate the baron, to admire his golden hair and godlike countenance, his crisp high shirt collar and flawless cravat, smoothly fitting blue cloth coat, snug fawn-colored pantaloons, gleaming hessian boots. "Fergus!" she breathed. "You came!"

Lady Amabel's appreciation of her good fortune, however belated, did much to console Lord Parrington for any previous neglect. "Hullo, Mab!" he said. "After your urgent letter, how could I stay away? In point of fact, I arrived yesterday."

"And you did not immediately come to see me?" Mab wore an enchanting pout. Then she recalled Eleanor's remark that Henrietta had been entertaining callers in the solar. "Oh! You *did!* And I was not here to greet you. How ungrateful you must have thought me—but I promise I was not!"

"I know you are not." Lord Parrington's presence in the solar at so very early an hour is readily explained: his parent also habitually rose late. *"I* don't think your manners lack polish. Neither will Mama, I'm sure, when she comes to realize you were engaged in consoling Lady March." He arched a brow. "What a mystery this is! Mama styles it the celebrated scandal of the disappearing Lord March."

Fergus's mama was a gorgon, Mab unkindly thought. "Your mama is also come to town?" she asked, as she sat down upon an embroidered chair.

"Naturally." Lord Parrington looked startled at the question. "She would not have liked to be left behind. I daresay it was due to the rigors of the journey that she was miffed by your seeming inattention—which is a thing no one could fairly blame in you, since Lady March was prostrate. Leave Mama to me! She will eventually come about."

Were Lady March prostrate, Mab reflected, it was not for the reasons envisioned by Lord Parrington; and were the baron's mama to become reconciled, ever, Mab would feast upon her tattered fan. That latter item she turned over in her hands. "If one may inquire?" Fergus delicately inserted. "Mab, *why* have you dust on your skirts and cobwebs in your hair?"

"Dust?" Lady Amabel glanced at her guilty skirts

58

and brushed hastily at her dark curls. "I was in the attics—Nell has taken a notion to investigate them, and I felt obliged to humor her! She is under a dreadful strain, poor thing!" Her latter statement was all too true, Mab mused. She narrowed her eyes, the better to observe Lord Parrington, who had withdrawn to the oriel window. "I don't suppose *you* know what happens to thieves?"

"Thieves?" Mab's abrupt switch of topic caused the baron to blink. "I'm happy to say I do not. Is *that* the dire event you hinted at in your letter? Have you been robbed, Mab? What a shocking thing."

Several things during this conversation with the object of her maidenly affections were to Mab coming clear. Fergus was not quite the cavalier imagination had painted him. This discovery was not surprising, since Mab knew the baron little better than many another modern damsel had known her prospective husband, lack of close acquaintance being in that day no good reason not to wed.

"Robbed?" she said vaguely. "Not a bit of it! I can't think where you took such a singularly foolish notion. Perhaps, Fergus, you might know something about how things are done at Bow Street?" She observed his indignant expression. "I should have known that you would not! I expect you number no magistrates among your acquaintance, either. A pity! I would have liked to ask—but never mind that!"

Perhaps his mama had not been wholly mistaken, decided Fergus, in her claim that Amabel's behavior merited reproof. From the nature of her queries, one might easily conclude that Mab was engaged in mischief of some sort. "You owe me an explanation," Lord Parrington said with grave propriety.

Lady Amabel eyed her caller's manly countenance, which was looking very solemn, and recalled that his mama was amazingly high in the instep—no fitting member of a conspiracy to outwit the forces of law, in short. There was little hope that anything she told Fergus would not be in turn related to his mama, Mab now

59

realized. "Where shall we live after we are married?" she asked abruptly. "I mean, what will happen to your mama?"

"Happen to her?" Fergus felt in some way that it was a trifle indelicate to discuss living arrangements before the knot was properly tied. Charitably, he made allowance for the strain imposed upon Mab by the misfortunes of her friends. The baron was not so very high a stickler as his mama, who was of the opinion that as result of these misfortunes Mab should give unfortunate Lady March the cut direct. "What *should* happen to her? Do you fear Mama will feel you have usurped her position? You need not! She will be happy to show you how to go on."

"I see." Mab could not imagine that Lady Katherine would be pleased to show any daughter-in-law anything other than how much she was disliked. Previously, Mab had not been aware of how firmly Lord Parrington remained tied to his mama's apron strings. Later, Mab would have to seriously ponder whether she wished to spend her married life with a gorgonish mama-in-law who would always be loading her with reproaches and pulling a long face.

"*Are* we to be married? I was under the impression your papa refused to give us his consent." Fergus moved from the oriel window to the chimney where Diana bathed. Once arrived there, he turned back to gaze suspiciously upon Mab. "The greatest wretch in nature—is *that* what you were talking about?"

How calmly he spoke of her impassioned letter—clearly, Lord Parrington was inclined toward no romantical high flights. Closeted alone with the young lady whom he wished to marry, a highly unusual circumstance, he had not uttered a single improper word, nor given the tiniest indication that he harbored any ardent thought. A young lady *might* be gratified by such restraint, Mab supposed. After witnessing high romance as enacted by Lord and Lady March, however, she was finding Fergus distinctly flat.

Mab tossed aside her fan and abandoned her chair.

"Perhaps I exaggerated a *trifle,* Fergus, but Papa had forbidden me to see you again, and I was feeling very out-of-sorts."

"Forbidden—" Lord Parrington gazed down upon the young lady who had joined him on the hearth. Mab was a very pretty damsel, he decided, even with dust smudged on her fair cheek and cobwebs in her dark hair. Any offspring of their union would have been attractive. However, there were in the world a great many other young women potentially capable of producing healthy, attractive offspring, young women whose papas weren't unalterably—and inexplicably—opposed to himself. "I am sorry to hear it. There remains nothing for us to do but say goodbye."

"Say *goodbye?* Just because Papa has taken one of his tweaks? I call that dashed poor spirited!" Lady Amabel's voice was very near a shriek. Upon espying the baron's horrified expression, she lowered it. "I crave forgiveness for ripping up at you, Fergus—not that it wasn't what you deserved!"

Though Lord Parrington was blessed not only with unusual beauty but also quickness of perception, he was at a loss to comprehend how his attitude displeased. This viewpoint he explained. To his explanation Lady Amabel reacted with a wrinkling of her pretty nose. "Papa decrees that we may not marry, and you intend to abide by his dictates! Have you not a ha'porth of spirit, Fergus? I think you must not. Had I realized how it is with you, I would never have run away!"

"You ran away," Fergus repeated slowly, as if to impress the magnitude of such arrant misconduct on a disbelieving brain. "How could you do such a thing? I am very disappointed in you, Mab. I can't imagine what Mama will say."

Lady Amabel gave not a button for Lady Katherine's prospective remarks. "If you do not think she'll like it, then don't tell her!" Mab snapped. "Save for Nell, and now you, no one knows that I ran away. Even Papa does not! And considering the state I found matters in

61

here, it's a very good thing I *did*, what with Nell being made to fret even worse by that odious Henrietta, not to mention Marriot!"

Not tell his mama of Amabel's misconduct? Here was a novel thought. Though Fergus was not certain of the propriety of withholding information from his parent, he foresaw that revelation could only lead to a further cutting up of his own peace. Fergus's peace was important to him. In part, his amiability resulted from a keen dislike of raised voices and hurtful accusations, as is sometimes the case.

Currently, it was Amabel's raised voice that he disliked. "Tell me, do you *really* want to join the militia?" he asked, and smiled.

Lady Amabel, who wished to quarrel no more than did Fergus, siezed gratefully upon this distraction. "Of course I do not!" she chided with twinkling eyes. "It was merely a means by which to distract Henrietta from Marriot. She is prone to go on at length in the most bloodcurdling manner. I wished to give her thoughts another direction." Her smile faded. "As you have sought to do with me, Fergus! Since you no longer wish to marry me, you may go away."

Could he have heard correctly? Had Amabel just *dismissed* him? It was a unprecedented situation for Lord Parrington, who was much more accustomed to being courted than given his congé. Perhaps she had not meant it? A quick glance at her stubborn expression convinced him that she had. "We must not be hasty!" he protested lamely.

"*I* am not hasty," responded Amabel with a sad little catch in her voice and a shocking disregard for the truth. "I am not the one who allows myself to be dictated to, who has not the least capability to manage my own affairs—" Prudently, Mab refrained from direct censure of the baron's dictatorial parent. "—the one who abandons his dearest friend *just* when she needs him most! But do not concern yourself, Fergus! We will not much longer be a household of defenseless women. Soon Marriot will come home."

"*Will* he, do you think?" Lord Parrington had not previously considered how difficult life must be for the ladies so mysteriously left behind.

Amabel lowered her gaze to the mantelpiece. "I'm sure of it! Why, I could tell you—but I must not! You do not like secrets! The thing is, once Marriot *does* return, he might be persuaded to put in a good word with Papa, who has always doted on him, and adjudged him up to all the rigs." Through her lashes, she peered at her companion. "I will tell you this much, Fergus. Marriot's absence has a *very* good explanation—but you must promise me not to breathe a word!"

As was not surprising in so cossetted a young gentleman, Lord Parrington secretly yearned after a more adventurous life. Could Mab's sudden interest in robberies and magistrates have to do with Lord March? he wondered. Could the vanished peer have run afoul of Bow Street?

If so, Fergus wanted no further part of the business. "You may trust me," he responded stiffly. "Upon my honor, Mab!"

Here was a pretty pickle; did she *not* reveal confidences, Lord Parrington would take offense. Unfortunately, Mab knew not what tale to tell, the explanation of Marriot's disappearance not having reached its final draft. She cast about in her mind. Nor was her ultimate utterance surprising in view of the recent invasion scares. Looking very conspiratorial, Mab leaned closer to the baron and breathed, "Spies!"

Spies? Whatever Fergus had expected, it was not that Lord March was involved in an attempt to thwart the ambitious Corsican. Indeed, so stunned was Fergus that he failed to wonder what the Emperor of the French had to do with thieves and magistrates and Bow Street. "Jupiter!" he gasped.

"Do not press me! I can say no more." Though Fergus had proven more gullible than she had anticipated— and a great deal less up to snuff!—Mab thought it would be foolish to press her luck. For that reason, she refrained from asking the baron's opinion of failing memories. Too, Mab was feeling a little lonely, as must any young lady disappointed in romance.

Perhaps there was yet hope for Fergus. Perhaps his apparent disinterest was merely result of a very high sense of decorum. "We are alone, Fergus!" she coyly pointed out.

Somewhat blankly, his thoughts still occupied with enemy agents, Lord Parrington gazed around the solar. "So we are. Ah, you mean that we should not be, and you are perfectly correct. Pray forgive me for placing you in so equivocal a position, Mab! I would not have done it for anything. You will permit me to take my leave."

The baron's leave-taking was not what Lady Amabel had in mind, as she quickly made apparent by clutching his coat-sleeve. Lord Parrington looked astonished by this temerity. "Gudgeon!" said Mab, though fondly. "I *meant* that you should kiss me!"

To this generous invitation, the baron returned a startled look, young ladies who invited gentlemen to kiss them not being something of which he had been brought up to approve. He did not long adhere to that lesson, however. "May I?" he echoed, staring fascinated into Mab's upturned face. Rosy-cheeked, she nodded. "*May* I, by Jove!"

It was, Lady Amabel decided, a very nice kiss, if hardly of the caliber recently—and frequently—bestowed upon one another by Lord and Lady March. One must bear in mind that years of practice had led to the expertise currently enjoyed by Marriot and Nell. Fergus showed promise of someday attaining a similar artistry, if only he could be pried out from beneath his mama's foot. Mab thought she would like to devote herself to that project, once this troublesome business of Marriot's was tidied up.

But of trouble Lady Amabel had as yet seen little, and one of its harbingers at that moment stepped into the solar. At the bacchanalian scene being there enacted, Henrietta gaped.

CHAPTER EIGHT

From the solar Lady Amabel proceeded next to the master bedchamber, where she scratched loudly at the door. When that portal opened, Mab dashed into the room, slammed the door shut behind her, and with her pretty person barred the entry, as if imminent invasion might be repulsed by outstretched arms and heaving breast.

"Gracious!" said Lady March, who wore a confection of cambric muslin held together by orchid ribbons, and over it the ancient fur cloak. "Whatever has happened to put you in such a tweak?"

"If you had discovered you had to live with Fergus's mama, you would be in a tweak also!" Mab sought to catch her breath. "She is a gorgon! A tartar! And what she will say to this piece of business, I shudder to think! If only your *odious* cousin had not stepped into the solar at *just* that moment—but it is too much to hope she will remain silent!"

"I fear you are correct. Henrietta has never remained silent about anything in all her life. Do you think you might tell me *what* we are talking about?"

Amabel looked rueful. "Have I not said? What a peagoose you must think me! But when I think of how *difficult* it was to persuade Fergus to kiss me, I vow I could spit nails!"

"He *kissed* you?" Lady March echoed, astonished. "Mab!"

"You must not censure him! Fergus is not in the petticoat-line, I assure you—indeed, he might never have kissed me at all, had I not intimated that he should." Mab sighed. "In point of fact, I had to ask him outright!"

"You had to—" In an attempt to clear up her confusion, Lady March shook her head, thus adding to the disorder of her chestnut locks, which were already in riotous disarray. "If your young man isn't, er, *romantic*, why are you so set on having him, Mab?"

"Had you ever seen Fergus," Mab said gloomily, "you would not ask me that. He is very near perfection—or would be if it were not for his gorgonish mama, who will doubtless make a piece of work about nothing— oh, blast! For Henrietta to step into the solar at *just* that moment was the unluckiest mischance!"

In a cravenly manner, Lady March reflected that she was very happy to have been spared the resultant kickup. "Poor Mab!" she sympathized. "Was it so very bad?"

"Bad?" Amabel's delightful features were chagrined. "I should say it was! There is a want of *openness* about my conduct, an *unsteadiness* of character—I am a harum-scarum young woman, *and* a hardened flirt! A wicked girl, she called me—*wicked!* How can you bear to have that sneaking gabble-grinder around you, Nell? She did not scruple to announce it her duty to tell Lady Katherine what has transpired—as if Fergus was a penny the worst of it! Oh, I do not mean to make a kickup, but I am *cursedly* provoked!"

"Perhaps she will reconsider," offered Lady March, without any real hope that Henrietta would bypass an opportunity to cast a blight upon Amabel's romance. "I might speak to her about it."

"You'll speak to her, I warrant!" Mab brushed futilely at the fur which had drifted from off the cloak onto her high-waisted, dust-smudged dress. "I'm surprised she hasn't already brought you the tale. Perhaps she knows I am here before her—or is composing Lady Katherine a note." Briefly, Mab looked hopeful. "I wonder if the old gorgon might think I've been compromised, in which event she would have to give us her blessing, so that her son's good name could be saved." Her spirits plummeted. "More likely she will decide I'm some scheming hussy who has led her son astray!"

Obviously some soothing comment was called for,

but Lady March could think of no hope she might hold out. "*I* will declare you have been compromised!" offered a deep voice from the depths of the formidable four-poster bedstead.

"You—" A sensible girl, Lady Amabel didn't for an instant think the bed had suddenly come to life, although she was so startled by this new entry into the conversation that her voice rose to a squeak. Should she swoon, she wondered—but this situation was fraught with possibilities too interesting to waste. "I thought I left you reading Torquenado's *Miracles*," she said sternly. "What are you doing in Nell's bed?"

In response to this singularly inappropriate question, which caused Lady March to turn very rosy, Lord March emerged from the depths of the old bedstead, and settled himself against one of the bone-inlaid posts. He wore a floor-length robe of expensive brocade, tied at the waist, and a self-satisfied smile. "I was so taken with the tale of the shipwrecked lady and her ape," he explained, "that I had to share it with Nell. Shall I cut up stiff about your treatment by young Parrington, brat? As head of the household in which you came perilously close to being seduced? A young girl under my protection? Oh, shame!"

"You are the one who should be ashamed, Marriot!" Though Lady March's tone was chiding, her expression was not. "You must not tease Mab. This unfortunate development can't enhance her position with Parrington's mama."

"Nothing could do that," Mab wryly pointed out, as she followed Lady March to the great bed, where Lord March was toying absently with her charming nightcap. "It's very kind of you to offer to help me, Marriot, but no one knows you *are* the head of the house!"

"They will soon enough." Lord March made room for his wife on one side of him, and Lady Amabel on the other, and shared the molting cloak among the three of them in an attempt at warmth. "I've decided my reappearance must be no longer delayed."

"Was *that* why you came down from the attic?" Mab

tried to imagine how it would feel to snuggle up to Fergus in this manner—without, of course, Nell on the other side. "Perhaps you should reconsider, Marriot. If the site of your reappearance is your wife's bedchamber, Henrietta is going to think it very odd."

"*Henrietta* is very odd." Thus Lord March disposed of his cousin. "So that we may be rid of her is one reason why I have decided to come out of hiding."

"It is a pity you didn't think of Henrietta in the first place!" Lady Amabel answered. "Once she was finished hauling me over the coals, she tried to interrogate me— as if *her* conduct was above reproach, which it isn't, because she didn't tell me Fergus and his mama had called. That is who you heard her talking to in the solar, Nell! And they came to see *me!* It is true, I assure you. Anyway, Henrietta is agog to discover why Marriot showed you a clean pair of heels, Nell. She said you would do better to prepare for tragedy than to rummage with me through the attics, and then she took to shuddering, and muttering about mice. I think it will be very *nice* when you reappear, Marriot, because Henrietta doesn't expect that you *will,* and her nose will be put out of joint!"

Lady March, gazing across her husband's enviable chest at Mab, glanced at the door. "Keep your voices down," she warned. "I wouldn't put it past Henrietta to eavesdrop."

"*Would* she?" Lord March succumbed to impulse, and nuzzled his wife's chestnut hair. "Listen at keyholes?"

"Certainly she would." Mab reclaimed Marriot's wandering attention by jabbing her elbow in his ribs. "She is a very rubbishing person, I think! But this is fair and far off. We must put our heads together—or rather, I wish the pair of you would *not* put your heads together because I am feeling oppressingly de trop."

Recalled to the unsatisfactory condition of her young friend's romance, Lady March raised herself from her husband's chest and patted his smooth cheek. "Poor Mab! We shall not allow Henrietta to cut up all your hopes."

Moved by this noble attitude, Lord March saluted his wife's hand. "No, we shan't," he said. "I'll send Henrietta packing, and demand that Parrington make reparations for the honor he has so carelessly besmirched. Will that suit you, brat?"

"Have you gone off your hinges?" Lady Amabel seriously doubted that anything would please her again. "Your own behavior is open to very unfavorable interpretations, Marriot! Nell, you need not be looking at me like a thundercloud! *I* did not say Marriot has done anything so dreadful—but we must not forget that he has lost his memory and *gained* what are likely stolen jewels."

So he had, and by this unpalatable reminder Lord and Lady March were reluctantly recalled to the present. Marriot gazed in a somber manner at the shabby valise which he had brought with him from the attic, as well as the Toledo walking sword. "If only I could remember!" he mourned.

"Oh, Marriot!" Eleanor's sigh was heartfelt.

"Well, you can't!" briskly interjected Mab. "And we can't simply wait until your memory returns, if ever it does. But you must have thought of some explanation for your absence, else you would not have left the attics. May we know what it is? Which reminds me, I had better tell you that I hinted to Fergus that you were involved in thwarting the French—don't frown at me, Nell! I didn't know what else *to* say!"

"By all means, don't scold Mab." Marriot gave his wife a little squeeze. "It isn't like you to kick up a dust over a trifle like espionage, puss! However, I fear that tale won't stand up to investigation—not that I am ungrateful, Mab!"

Lady Amabel contemplated giving his lordship's ribs another jab. "It is not kind of you to *gammon* me," she said sternly. "I am devilish out of humor, and so would you be, had you had your odious Cousin Henrietta ripping up at you about bacchanalian scenes."

Lord March wondered what his odious cousin would think could she but see him at this moment, disposed regally in the middle of the ornate four-poster, wrapped in furs, with a lovely lady on each side. Doubtless the sight—or her own indelicate deductions—would inspire her to apoplexy. Hopefully, Marriot eyed the door.

Unacquainted with his lordship's own indelicate thoughts, Amabel continued to speak. "I can understand why you wouldn't care to say you'd been involved with enemy agents, or even tinkers, or a press gang— and Nell wouldn't like it to be said you'd eloped with another female. But we must say you were *somewhere*—I do wish you would cease gazing at Nell in that *mawkish* manner, Marriot!"

Lord March, who looked not the least mawkish, despite Lady Amabel's unkind accusations, removed his fond gaze from his wife's patrician face. "I wish you would try to be a little more understanding, brat! How would you feel if you hadn't seen young Parrington for six months?"

Mab would not see Fergus for a great deal longer than six months, she thought, did his mama's will prevail. She drew a deep breath, inhaled a quantity of the fur which wafted richly through the air, and sneezed. "Would you mind," she gasped, when she had caught her breath, "having been kidnapped?"

"Kidnapped?" Lady March's voice was horrified. "Mab!"

"Imagine how I must have felt!" Lord March threw himself into this new rôle. "Alone and ailing—of course I must have been ailing, else I could easily have overpowered my captors, all of them!—without wifely sympathy or succor."

"Nell! Do you succor Marriot at this moment, I vow I shall wash my hands of you both!" To emphasize her displeasure, Mab gave a little bounce. "You seem to have forgotten that the tale must satisfy *both* Henrietta and Bow Street. Though I do not know a great deal about such things, I conjecture that the runner who could not find you will want to know where you've been."

"I thought of that." Marriot smiled at Lady Amabel's

impatient expression. "You must not be cross with me, Mab; I have been thinking very hard of a reasonable explanation of why I hopped the twig—departed so suddenly, that is! And I have decided I must have gone to Cornwall."

"Cornwall?" Eleanor looked mystified. *"Why?"*

"Because I had to go *some*where, puss, and Cornwall is further away than most. We do have holdings there." He shifted position, between the cloak and the ladies having grown quite warm. "I suppose you will ask me why I embarked upon such a journey in the middle of the night."

Now that Lord March had withdrawn his manly presence, lounging instead amid the pillows at the head of the large bed, Lady March and Lady Amabel were left to huddle together beneath the cloak. Neither found this activity half so satisfying as when Marriot had lent them his lean bulk. "I *wouldn't* ask that," said Mab, after judicious thought. "Nor would anyone else who knew you, Marriot! Don't get on your high ropes, Nell! You cannot deny that Marriot gets absentminded when he's had a drop too much to drink. To use the word with no bark on it, there is no telling what he'll do when he's three parts disguised! It would be just like him to set off for Cornwall in the middle of the night, without luggage—and without letting you know!"

"That may be." A trifle sulkily, Lady March pushed back her tousled locks. "But it would *not* be like him to forget to send me word for six months!"

"Perhaps I *did* send word, but it went astray." Lord March sought a comfortable position against the high, intricately carved headboard. "The advantage of this particular explanation is that the servants can be instructed what to say. Personally, I would prefer to say as little as possible." He looked at the valise. "Unfortunately, a mysterious silence would not satisfy Bow Street."

"Or Cousin Henrietta," added Nell drily. Though Eleanor would have infinitely preferred to keep her husband safe in the attic room, she realized Marriot would be miserable locked away. Too, there were advantages to having a spouse in residence. She blushed. "Why did you go to Cornwall, Marriot?"

"Business called him," suggested Mab, inspired by a nibbled knuckle. "Perhaps a dishonest bailiff who absconded with some revenues—perhaps Marriot was so displeased that he personally tracked down the culprit. No, that won't fadge; if Marriot did apprehend the bailiff, the man would have to go to gaol, and I do not think we will persuade any of your servants to be put in prison merely to add credence to our tale! Maybe you were in an accident, Marriot, and your senses were disordered—you lay for days in a high fever, raving, within inches of losing your life!"

"High flights!" Lord March did not look especially thrilled by this highly dramatic theory of what had chanced. "It would be quite an accident that left me incapacitated for six months."

Lady Amabel, who now had the fur cloak all to herself, looked meaningfully upon Lord and Lady March, both of whom were currently arranged comfortably amid the pillows against the intricately carved headboard. "I think it *must* have been quite an accident!" she remarked.

Marriot grimaced. "Point taken, brat! The thing is, we must have an explanation that gives rise to the *least* speculation and comment. I do not care to have anyone delve too deeply into my activities these last months, especially since I don't know what they were."

"Oh, Marriot!" Having come across her nightcap, Eleanor set it back upon her curls. "Perhaps we should give this notion up—at least wait until it is *safer* for you to reveal yourself."

"Puss, it may never be safe." Lord March assisted his wife's efforts with the nightcap. "We don't know how I came by those accursed jewels, but *some*one must—and if that someone is to enlighten us, I must make an appearance."

Lady March was doubtful. "It sounds dangerous."

Before Lord March could respond with appreciation

to his wife's concern for his well-being, Lady Amabel interrupted. "You do not like my explanation for your absence," she said crossly. "Pray, Marriot, what tale do you mean to tell?"

"The obvious one." Very tenderly, Lord March gazed upon his wife's face. "Unless Nell would mind it dreadfully, I think we will have quarreled."

CHAPTER NINE

Not much later that same day, the astonishing tale of Lord March's reappearance had already gotten round. Currently, the chief source of this news broadcast was holding forth in London's largest bookshop, Mr. Lackington's Temple of the Muses in Finsbury Square. "Quarreled! Can you credit it? And all this time she allowed me to go on thinking he'd been kidnapped by tinkers, or taken by a press gang!"

Henrietta did not lack for an audience, comprised not wholly of the person to whom she spoke. Books and periodicals had little power to interest those elegant browsers fortunate enough to be within earshot. "Stab me!" returned Lady Katherine, who was this day bundled up in a quantity of black wool topped by a bonnet of purple velvet covered with lace, trimmed with purple ribbons, and finished off with a short lace veil. "Here's a pretty business!"

To this encouraging display of interest, Henrietta responded with a smirk. "You do not know the half of it!" For that matter, neither did Henrietta, which was a source of considerable chagrin. Especially, Henrietta was curious about the cause of Marriot's quarrel with Eleanor, a quarrel which had taken him to the wilds of Cornwall. "Take my word for it! There's more here than meets the eye."

Lady Katherine was perfectly content to accept Henrietta's account of her cousin's homecoming, as were those other individuals so fortunate as to have chosen to wander this day through the Temple's aisles. "Plague on't, stop shilly-shallying!" demanded Lady Katherine, whose interest in the celebrated scandal of the disappearing Lord March was not one whit diminished by the fact she'd never set eyes on the gentleman in all her life. "Tell how this miracle came about."

Unaccustomed to being the center of attention, even the vituperative attention of a Lady Katherine, Henrietta smoothed her three-quarter length pelisse of plush, a shaggy cotton velvet with a long nap resembling fur, which she wore over a simple walking dress. Upon her wispy hair was a helmet hat made of willow with a military feather over the crown. *"Well?"* demanded Lady Katherine.

Henrietta started, setting her feather atremble. "Marriot has been in Cornwall—something to do with his holdings there and a bailiff who turned out to be less honest than he should—I do not know the whole of it, because the Towers is at sixes and sevens, as you might imagine—although Marriot professes himself displeased with all the fuss."

Lady Katherine was stricken with a similar dissatisfaction, result of her informant's paucity of detail. "Faith! What about the quarrel with his wife?"

Henrietta's awe of her companion was in no way lessened by this display of vulgar curiosity; Henrietta liked nothing better than to have a cozy chat with someone as fond of tittle-tattle as herself. Unfortunately, she could not provide enlightenment. "I do not know!" she sighed. "Whatever it was about must have been very dreadful, to cause Marriot to set out for Cornwall in the middle of the night."

Lady Katherine's raddled face was avid. She leaned closer, balancing on her cane. "Do you think she—er?" she delicately asked.

"'Er'?" Henrietta looked puzzled. "Ah! No, I don't think it. At least she hasn't while *I* have been at Marcham Towers—I do assure you that, had Eleanor's affection strayed, I would know! That is what has me in such a puzzle. When I asked Marriot why he had chosen such a queer way to go about his business, he said he must have been three parts disguised!"

Lady Katherine pursed her bloodless lips. "Is the man a drunkard?" she inquired.

"A—" Henrietta would allow no outsider to serve her family up as gossip fodder, fond as she herself might be of tossing out the occasional juicy tidbit. "Nothing of the sort! It is merely that Marriot does *not* have a hard head, and when he drinks more than is prudent—which he does not do often!—his thinking goes astray. Or so Eleanor has it! *I* would not be surprised if he returned home in that condition, because he did so in the same manner as he left, in the middle of the night!" People were making a habit of midnight arrivals, Henrietta reflected; first Mab, now Marriot. Every instinct hinted that mischief was afoot at Marcham Towers. The precise nature of that mischief, Henrietta could not guess, but she did not intend to budge an inch before she found out. "Last night Marriot certainly was not in residence—yet when I went to see Elinor this morning after I had dispatched my note to you, there he was!"

"After?" Lady Katherine's attention had been caught by a discrepancy in the chronology of Henrietta's account. "If you didn't mean to tell me March had returned, what was the purpose of this meeting to be? It had better be good, Dougharty! To be out in this abominable weather is *not* what I can like!"

Lady Katherine had liked it well enough only moments past, reflected Henrietta, her military feather trembling anew with the force of the reprimand. Nonetheless, that reprimand did not long deflate her spirits. Denied the opportunity to console Eleanor for tragic tidings of her husband, Lady Katherine would make an excellent second best. Not that Lady Katherine's lamented spouse had indulged in shockingly irregular conduct. A pity the same could not be said about her son! "You must prepare yourself," Henrietta said with relish, "to hear very bad news."

"Bad news?" Lady Katherine snapped. "What the deuce are you prosing on about, Dougharty?"

There were few things Henrietta enjoyed better than to let drop dire hints. *"Never* has there been anything equal to it!" she prophesied in tones of doom.

"Equal to *what?*" Lady Katherine did not care to be made participant in a cat-and-mouse game. Irritably, she raised her cane.

Though Henrietta flinched, she would not be balked of her triumph. "We must be discreet!" she murmured, looking sharply around. "One does not know *whom* one may trust, what with all these robberies—not that I have anything worth stealing, but it doesn't hurt to take precautions, all the same! That is why I wished to meet you here instead of at Marcham Towers. Not that we might not be robbed, of course, but so we might not be overheard!"

Lady Katherine considered it most likely that they would be overheard in the Temple, so thick was the press of people in the aisles. This contradictory viewpoint she promptly put forth.

"Oh yes! I do not doubt it!" Henrietta responded serenely. "But we shall not be overheard by Mab."

As result of this simple statement, Lady Katherine experienced a sinking sensation in her midriff. "Stab me!" she said.

"I feel for you, Lady Katherine!" Henrietta's glance was sympathetic. "*Truly* I do! To discover in such a manner that your own son—oh dear, oh dear! I promise you I doubted the fidelity of my own eyes."

Her companion would no longer have a problem with her vision, Lady Katherine thought grimly, did she succumb to the impulse to scratch out those sharp orbs. "Discover *what,* and in what manner?" she snapped. "In plain English, if you please!"

Henrietta *did* please; seldom was opportunity granted her to strike such a blow. "I fear your son has fallen victim to Lady Amabel," she confided. "Unless he goes about kissing young females as a matter of habit, he *must!*"

"Goes about—" In an attempt to avoid swooning from the shock of the intelligence that her son was earning some notoriety as a philanderer, Lady Katherine groped for her vinaigrette. "There is some mistake!"

"None at all, I promise you!" Henrietta had the temerity to pat Lady Katherine's hand. "I walked in on them embracing—it was in the solar. Such a distasteful business! I would not have expected such goings-on, even from Lady Amabel. So you may be sure I told her, and read her a *very* stern scold."

A scold was far too mild a retribution for the young lady who had left Lady Katherine's son debauched. "That scheming hussy!" moaned Lady Katherine into her vinaigrette. "She has led my poor lamb astray! Never have I been so dismayed!"

"Of course you have not." During moments of disaster, especially disasters of her own devising, Henrietta was at her best. "Anyone must have been disgusted with Amabel's conduct, and so I told her, and so I *feel!* Even though your son seemed to feel that *I* should come under the gravest censure for having intervened. Meddling, he called it—but I do not hold it against him! Between you and me, Lady Katherine, I suspect I arrived in the very nick of time!"

Lady Katherine did indeed in that moment resemble a gorgon, one of those snake-haired sisters whose terrific aspect turned beholders to stone. "The nick of time!" she echoed. "Has it gone so far as *that?*"

"No." Henrietta was very sorry to admit that it had not. "But there is no saying it might not have! Clearly Lady Amabel is no better than one of the wicked, else she would not have lured your son into a squalid little debauch. This is such a dreadful business! You have my utmost sympathy."

Lady Katherine was in much greater need of a means of revenge, some method by which Amabel's presumption might be repaid. How *dared* the minx cast out lures to Fergus—and how dared *he* rise to the bait? Lady Katherine would have several sharp words to say to her offspring regarding his newly developed penchant for amorous vagaries. In such a dreadful manner Lady Katherine glowered that the aisles closest to the ladies were rapidly cleared.

"I won't have it!" For emphasis, Lady Katherine

78

pounded her cane on the floor. "I won't have it, do you hear?"

Henrietta could hardly have failed to do so, along with anyone else in the bookshop; the proprietor himself came forward to ascertain who was assaulting his floor. As result of this intervention, Lady Katherine limped haughtily to the door. "Curst busybodies!" growled Lady Katherine, as they passed outside.

Henrietta did not think her companion referred to themselves. "What will you do?" she asked. "It is no good applying to Eleanor or Marriot regarding Amabel; they are a great deal too wrapped up in themselves." And very queer it was that they should be so affectionate, she thought. Marriot's homecoming was very warm for a fellow who had disappeared for quite six months following a quarrel. "And I fear that Amabel herself showed not the slightest remorse, or intention of mending her wicked ways."

"She'll mend them, or I'll know the reason why she doesn't!" Lady Katherine's ruined face was a study in mingled outrage and chagrin. "But I shall have to be very subtle. I think I must require your assistance in this matter, Dougharty—fiend sieze the wench!"

CHAPTER TEN

While Lady Katherine was pulling a long face over Henrietta's accounting of Lord Parrington's misdeeds, and both dowagers were heartily wishing Lady Amabel to perdition, Mab was putting Henrietta's absence to very good account. At this particular moment, she was fluttering her eyelashes in a wholly outrageous manner. "You could not stay away!" she murmured, highly gratified. "*I* know how it is! But I would not wish to get you in trouble with your mama."

"If you did not wish to land me in the briars, you shouldn't have asked me to kiss you!" he snapped.

This was no loverlike tone, surely? Mab's long lashes ceased to flutter, and she blinked. Perhaps Fergus was merely ill at ease? She giggled. "I know what will cheer you! We will enact another bacchanalian scene!"

Lord Parrington did not find this sally amusing. "No, we shan't!" he retorted, and for good measure fell back a pace. "Am I not already in difficulties enough? When I think what Mama will have to say—she will be devilish out of humor. My thoughts are of the most desponding cast."

Mab thought it must be obvious to even the most casual observer that the baron was in the dumps. Lady Amabel peered through her long lashes at Lord Parrington. Herself resourceful, Mab had little patience with young men who shilly-shallied around the helm of their own ship of fate. "Fergus," she said bluntly, "if you did not wish to see me, why the blazes did you come to Marcham Towers?"

It occurred to the baron that he'd been less than diplomatic. "Naturally I wish to see you," he responded, in tones that were as unenthusiastic as they were polite. "But the *purpose* of my visit was to speak with that female who burst in on us—the bosom-bow of my mama's! What was her name? Dougharty?"

Definitely there was a craven streak in Lord Parrington, Mab decided sadly, else he would not lower himself to try and turn Henrietta up sweet. He thought to persuade Henrietta not to relate his transgressions to Lady Katherine. Mab derived a certain perverse satisfaction from informing the baron he had come too late.

"Too late!" Fergus blanched. "Say you're bamming me, Mab. Admit it, there's a good girl!"

"But I'm not." In proportion to Lord Parrington's unease, Lady Amabel's patience grew short. "Henrietta has gone to report your misconduct to your mama. Good God, Fergus, you have put yourself in a regular taking over this business. What do you think she may do to you? You are a grown man!"

Not surprisingly, this unsympathetic attitude did nothing to reconcile its target with its source. "Mama will not do anything *to* me," Fergus responded stiffly, "except fly into the boughs and make a dreadful kickup. *No* one can raise a dust like Mama, as you would know, had you ever seen her in a pelter—and you may be grateful you have not." Were there justice in the world, it would be Mab who suffered his parent's wrath, Fergus silently added. Was not this cursed business her fault?

Happily, Lord Parrington kept this last reflection silent, else Lady Amabel might have grown so exasperated that she box his ears. As it was, she barely refrained. "You had better come in and meet Marriot," she said repressively, and gestured toward the door of the solar. "Since you're here. Do not raise your brows at me, Fergus! I assure you Marriot is within, and Nell also. Believe me, I have no more desire than you for another tête-à-tête." So saying, she swept before him into the solar.

Lord Parrington did not *dis*like the notion of further tête-à-tête, precisely; the disruption of his last such encounter had only temporarily soured him on romance. No opportunity being given him to explain these nuances of sentiment, he followed Lady Amabel into the solar. Lord March was indeed present, as Mab had promised, and Fergus was privileged to make the acquaintance of this mysteriously disappearing and reappearing gentleman, who was dressed casually in a morning coat of superfine with plated buttons, buckskin breeches, boots with wide turnover tops of light brown. "Hallo, Parrington!" said Lord March. "So you are the young man who's leading our Mab astray."

"Oh no, Marriot!" With an unfriendly glance at Fergus, Mab resumed her place beside Lord March on the chocolate red daybed, where before the baron's arrival she had been receiving instruction in how to play macao. "It is *I* who have led Fergus astray. Perhaps we must assure him that I did so in a brief fit of madness—which has since passed."

"Ah. It was a misunderstanding." Lord March cast an experienced eye on Mab's sulky face. "We shall say no more of it. Least said, soonest mended, brat!"

Thus reminded of the sometimes unfortunate results of her hasty temper, Lady Amabel returned Lord March's glance. Ruefully, she smiled. "That's the ticket!" said his lordship, and gave her a little hug.

Lady March, meanwhile observing Lord Parrington, understood why Mab considered the baron an Adonis—certainly he was very near perfection, at least in form. Eleanor was considerably more interested, however, in substance. She suspected, from Lord Parrington's frigid demeanor, that his nature was cold. But Mab must be the best judge of who she wished to kiss. Since Mab in these moments did not seem to care to converse with the baron, let alone kiss him, Nell stepped forward. "May I offer you some refreshment?" she inquired.

"Thank you, no!" Fergus was relieved to be diverted from the spectacle of Mab rubbing shoulders with Lord March—Marriot's charm was as palpably experienced by members of his own sex as the opposite, and consequently Fergus was piqued. March was deucedly friendly with Mab, the baron thought. He also thought it very strange that Lady March didn't seem to mind. "I called in hopes of persuading your cousin not to repeat, er, certain erroneous impressions she had received."

"I am so sorry!" Lady March indicated that Lord Parrington should be seated in one of the lavishly embroidered chairs. "Henrietta has a disposition to meddle, I fear. It is the result of not having enough worthwhile things to occupy her time." Nell paused, then her crooked smile flashed. "I will be frank! Formality would be foolish, when you have been pitchforked willy-nilly into our affairs. Henrietta takes every pleasure in setting people at loggerheads."

This blunt disclosure, while not relieving his apprehensions, did prompt Lord Parrington to award his hostess a second, closer glance. She was a well-setup female, he discovered, though not so flamboyantly attractive as Lady Amabel. Mab currently not standing high in his favor, Fergus found much to admire in Eleanor's muslin gown with elbow sleeves and pearl buttons, her paisley shawl with amber tones, even the classical coils in which she wore her chestnut hair. "These last months will have been difficult for you," he remarked. "You will be glad that Lord March has come home."

"Oh, yes!" Lady March's expression, as she turned toward her spouse, was very fond—*so* fond that Fergus found it in himself to pity her because Lord March was intent on Lady Amabel. Lady March was too unworldly to realize that a blatant flirtation was being carried on right under her nose. Thought of such an innocent enduring the abuses of a gazetted philanderer—for no one but a philanderer would turn that irresistible charm upon any lady other than his wife—wrenched the baron's heart. Or perhaps Lady March *did* realize her husband's perfidy and chose to put a good face on it. Here was a female worthy of a gentleman's highest regard—one, moreover, with troubles worse even than his own.

Unaware of the rôle assigned her by Lord Parrington, Nell could not imagine what caused that young man to stare. She decided he must be curious about Marriot's reappearance, as who would not. "My husband has been in Cornwall—I fear his bailiff had absconded with some revenues—too, we had had a difference of opinion—" Lord Parrington's sympathetic expression caused Nell a guilty pang, and her voice trailed off. How she loathed deception! But she would loathe it even more were Marriot taken as a thief. "But nothing to signify!"

Doubtless that difference of opinion had concerned a woman, thought Lord Parrington; perhaps even Mab. "Of course it does not signify. All that must matter to you now is your husband's return." Fergus frowned. "Then it was not true when Amabel hinted that enemy agents were concerned."

"Enemy agents?" Lady March recalled Mab's tale. "No, it was not. I am sorry to say it, but Mab's fondness for adventure sometimes leads her to say things she should not. Doubtless Mab would have liked it very well had Marriot become involved with spies and smugglers, but I assure you Marriot would not have liked it at all!" Her expression was amused. "My husband is no corsair."

Lord Parrington, watching Lady March's husband attempt to teach Lady Amabel macao, suspected Lord March was a great deal more adventurous than his wife thought. Certainly Mab seemed to be enjoying her game very well; scarce a moment passed that she didn't giggle or flutter her eyelashes or blush. "You must not hold Mab's impulsiveness against her!" Lady March added. "She means no harm by it."

Nor did a carrier of the plague mean harm, reflected Fergus, and lack of intention did not lessen the number of death carts. *Not* that he suspected Lady Amabel had dealt him a fatal blow. In the coolest of manners, Lord Parrington had decided it was time he fix his affections, and had settled upon Mab as a suitable wife. Now he began to wonder if his mama had been correct in claiming the hour was *un*ripe.

84

Lady March could not help but be aware that her visitor labored under some strong emotion, though she could not guess at the considerations which exercised his mind. In point of fact, Lady March would have been surprised at those considerations, for Fergus did not give the appearance of a young man experiencing grave self-doubts. For the first time made aware that he possessed other than sterling qualities, young Lord Parrington was responding with near revulsion, and for his divergence from his usual unexceptionable behavior he unhesitatingly blamed Mab. Fergus had never dreamed of ripping up at elderly ladies, or withholding things from his mama, before Mab's entrance into his life.

His impeccable manners had deserted him along with his usual good humor, Fergus realized; as result of his continued silence, Lady March was looking very puzzled. Fergus cast about in his mind for an innocuous topic of conversation, one that would involve neither profligate peers nor impulsive misses. "Even though your husband was not engaged with enemy agents, we may be sure others have been!"

Though the antics of the Corsican's hirelings were not something with which Lady March usually concerned herself—Lady March had had much more immediate troubles these last several months—she gallantly tried for an appropriate response. "Mab thinks women should be permitted to join the militia!" Nell offered weakly. Retorted Lord Parrington in an ungallant manner, "Mab would!"

Lady March had become aware that young Lord Parrington had not the aspect of a young man very far gone in infatuation, as Nell had assumed must be the condition of any gentleman kissed by Mab. In fact, Lord Parrington had done no more than render the merest observances of civility—to Mab, at least—while in this room. Had they quarreled? wondered Nell. And then she wondered, somewhat indelicately, why Mab had wished to kiss the baron in the first place. Still, Mab *had* wished it, else she would not have done it. Perhaps

85

there was something Nell could do to set her friend's interrupted romance aright.

Enemy agents and the militia having served him poorly, Lord Parrington sought some alternate topic. It would not do for Mab to realize her perfidy had left him feeling like a leaden lump. Why was it he had never before realized Mab *was* a dreadful flirt, just like his mama had claimed? She was so busy with Lord March that she had no thought to spare himself. Some marital bliss he might look forward to! thought Fergus. A wife whose flirtatious glances were directed ever elsewhere. "What think you of Bonaparte's coronation, ma'am?" he asked.

"Hmm?" Lady March was pondering the means by which she might best assist romance. "The coronation? I was not there. Oh! You mean, what do I think of what I've heard? I have heard very little about it, in truth. Henrietta has had a great deal to say on the subject, being an avid reader of the newssheets, but I have not paid her the heed I ought."

"You have had other things with which to concern yourself." Lord Parrington promptly set himself to remedy Lady March's abysmal ignorance of the monumental events which had lately transpired in the world.

To Lord Parrington's attempts at enlightenment, Eleanor paid scant heed, though at some other time she might have been very well entertained by his account of the five-hour long coronation procession, and the ceremony which took place in Notre Dame.

When the baron's voice trailed off, Eleanor roused. "You will think me a poor sort of hostess!" she apologized. "I fear I am that. Pray forgive my inattention. There is a great deal on my mind—not that it excuses my air-dreaming!"

"Do not regard it," responded Fergus, ever kind.

Dared she ask outright if Lord Parrington and Mab had quarreled? Nell glanced at the baron's godlike countenance, and in its marble immobility found very good reason why she should not. Yet one wished to do *some*thing to right whatever has gone amiss. Then

86

there was the ever-present puzzle of how Marriot had spent his six-month absence. Eleanor sighed.

Lady March had good reason for preoccupation, decided Fergus, chiefly her husband's blatant flirtation with a scheming little minx. Lord Parrington experienced another compassionate pang. "I must take my leave of you," he murmured. "I will have to render my apologies to your cousin some other time."

"You mean to apologize to Henrietta?" Eleanor looked startled. "Whatever for? Perhaps I should not say so, but it sounds to me like Henrietta should apologize to *you!*"

"No, no!" Lord Parrington hoped he was gentleman enough to admit when he was wrong. "I spoke much more sharply to her than she deserved."

In Eleanor's opinion, no one could speak more sharply than Henrietta deserved. "As you wish," she said doubtfully. "Henrietta will be sorry that she wasn't here to receive you herself."

"I don't doubt it." Few knew better than Fergus how elderly female minds worked. "Though the circumstances of our meeting have not been auspicious, I hope you will not hold it against me, Lady March. If you should not mind it, I would like to call on you again."

Call on *her?* Eleanor was puzzled until she realized the baron sought an unexceptionable excuse to visit Mab. His mama must be quite a tartar, Nell decided. "We would be pleased," she replied. Satisfied, for he had formed the noble intention of consoling Lady March for her husband's neglect, as well as the ignoble intention of giving Mab a sorely deserved set down, Fergus took his leave.

Satisfied though Lord Parrington may have been with the outcome of his visit, others were a great deal less. No sooner had the door closed behind the baron than Lady Amabel cast herself upon Lady March's chest and burst into noisy tears.

CHAPTER ELEVEN

Due to these developments, as well as her ever-present concern for Marriot, Lady March's spirits were not greatly improved the next day. Nor were the efforts of her companion directed toward that goal. Henrietta might have expressly sought to do the opposite. "I do not stand on ceremony with you, Eleanor!" she uttered. "You must perceive that to leave any gentleman alone with that young woman is to *invite* disgrace!"

Lady March scowled at her reflection in a plate glass shop window. "Henrietta," she said untruthfully, "I have not the most distant guess what you are talking about!"

Why Eleanor was frowning in that dreadful fashion at her own image, Henrietta did not know. Had *she* been decked out in such a pretty conversation hat—a sarcenet confection lined with silk and crowned with flowers, which covered one ear and tied under the chin with blue ribbons—she would have been feeling quite top of the trees. And had she been privileged to wear a walking dress with a gathered flounce above the hem, and a military pelisse—alas, poor relations possessed no such stylish things.

"I am talking about Lady Amabel." Henrietta's lack of material possessions was compensated for by her ability to spread discontent. "I most earnestly conjure you to keep a close eye on that girl. Your fondness blinds you to her faults, I think, else you would not have left her behind with Marriot."

"Left her—" Lady March stared. "Have you windmills in your head, Henrietta? Marriot has known Mab from the cradle."

"Tut!" Such staggering naiveté caused Henrietta to shake her head. "That makes it all the worse. You must not permit yourself to be blinded by affection, Eleanor, although it is to your credit that you do not wish to think poorly of the chit."

Lady March's thoughts regarding her companion, on the other hand, did her no credit at all. Only this reflection enabled Nell to swallow Henrietta's strictures with a semblance of good grace. "You are making a piece of work about nothing. I wish to hear no more of this."

"But, Eleanor, you must!" Henrietta was in the habit of considering no wishes above her own. "Else you find yourself again left wondering when—if!—your husband will come home. Anyone must see how it is with you and Marriot, even if you do not choose to tell me exactly why you quarreled. Odd that we did not suspect earlier—but sometimes these tendencies do not become apparent until mid-life!"

Lady March had rapidly come to regret the generous impulse which had prompted her to ask Henrietta's company on this foray into Oxford Street. She would much rather have remained in Marcham Towers, where Marriot and Mab had progressed from vingt-et-un to hazard and faro and other games of pure chance. Yet if she had stayed within doors, then Henrietta would have also, thereby cutting up everyone's peace. *"What* tendencies do you accuse Marriot of belatedly displaying?" she inquired crossly. "I warn you, Henrietta, that I do not care for this farrago of nonsense!"

"Of course you do not!" Henrietta looked arch. "But I could never forgive myself if I did not drop a gentle hint. You are very unworldly, are you not, dear Eleanor? Not that I mean to suggest you should be any other thing! Those of us who have had to make our own way, as it were, learn very quickly to recognize a spade, and to call it by name! In short, I fear that Lady Amabel's *scruples* are not what they should be."

If only Mab could be persuaded to be conciliating, or Henrietta more forebearing—but Mab and Henrietta held each other in equally keen dislike. "Fudge!"

retorted Eleanor, who was more disposed to take Mab's behalf. "I never heard anything half so absurd."

"Absurd, you call me?" Henrietta's plump cheeks turned pink. "When you discover Lady Amabel kissing Marriot you may change your mind!"

"When I discover—" The novelty of this suggestion caused Eleanor to pause mid-stride. "Henrietta," she chuckled, "you are a *goose!* Mab and Marriot are friends. You must not suspect poor Mab of being a co-quette just because you happened to see her kiss Lord Parrington. Most young ladies *would* like to kiss Par-rington, I imagine. Mab was merely resourceful enough to *do* it! If behavior is to be censured, Henrietta, yours was worse than Mab's. All *she* did was kiss a young man for whom she feels a deep affection. *You* were the one who carried tales."

As is not unusual among those who ascribe to plain dealing, Henrietta did not like that practice applied to herself. "Well!" she gasped.

"No, *not* well!" Lady March abandoned herself to the ill humor attendant upon her cousin's countless spiteful remarks. "In point of fact, it was very ill done. Mab does not deserve that you should seek to do her so poor a turn, nor I daresay does Parrington. He seemed a perfectly unexceptionable, amiable young man. Yet you must do your utmost to pose them difficulties. Hen-rietta, I wish you would not be so *busy* about other people's affairs! But I did not mean to scold you. We will say no more of it." She directed Henrietta's atten-tion to a shop window displaying silks and muslins and calico, then to a plumassier's stock of fancy feathers and artificial flowers, and at last led her into the Pan-theon Bazaar.

Though Henrietta was not in the habit of dagger drawing with those beneath whose roof she sojourned, she did not kindly accept criticism from any source. "You seem to have a high opinion of Lord Parrington," she remarked, laying Eleanor's unkind words smack at Lady Amabel's door.

"I do." Lady March was relieved that Henrietta did

not mean to sulk. "He seemed very unassuming and polite. In addition to being handsome as an Adonis!" Privately, Nell thought Mab's papa hadn't been far off the mark when he called the baron a popinjay. Still one could not fairly censure a young man for being a trifle *too* cool and polite. "Indeed, I doubt there is anything in Parrington *to* disapprove."

Here was high praise! As she judiciously fingered some cottage twill, Henrietta wondered what it meant. Perhaps she had been mistaken in assuming that Eleanor's devotion to Marriot was complete. Perhaps Eleanor *had,* or was at least tempted to—Parrington *was* very attractive, and there was a scant couple years difference in their ages—Gracious! Little wonder, did the wind blow in this direction, that Eleanor had not hesitated to leave Marriot alone with the flirtatious Lady Amabel. Were her husband lured into an entanglement, Eleanor could pursue inclination with a guiltless conscience. Henrietta dropped the cottage twill and turned upon Lady March a horrified glance.

"I hope that now you don't mean to tell me Parrington is also to be censured!" protested Nell upon glimpsing Henrietta's Friday face. "Because I do not wish to hear any such thing. And since I have given Parrington leave to call on us, you may as well reconcile yourself to his frequent presence in Marcham Towers—yes, and I must have your word that you will cease to publish the details of our daily existence to the world!"

With this last ungenerous accusation, Henrietta could not fairly quarrel; it was largely due to her efforts that so many rumors and speculations had greeted Marriot's return. By the indication that her suspicions were not without foundation, however, Henrietta was both horrified and thrilled. One did not *wish* disgrace to descend upon one's family—but if Lady Katherine had been overset by the intelligence that Lady Amabel had kissed Fergus, the intelligence that Nell contemplated doing likewise would render her prostrate. "Gracious!" Henrietta said aloud.

Already regretting her hasty words, Lady March

gazed in a somewhat gloomy manner upon a pair of elegant French gloves. "We understand each other, I think," she added somewhat lamely. "Now let us talk of other things."

Understood each other? Henrietta fancied she understood Eleanor very well indeed. Amabel wasn't the only female who hankered after Lord Parrington. Nell would like to be equally resourceful. Perhaps it was not Marriot whose misconduct had sparked the quarrel which had resulted in his disappearance. Perhaps it was Eleanor who was at fault.

"Why are you staring at me in that exceedingly odd manner?" plaintively inquired Lady March. "If I have wounded your sensibilities, I am sorry for it, but there were things that needed to be said. Now tell me your preference as regards these gloves!"

That matter at length settled, as result of which Nell became possessor of a pair of gloves she neither needed nor liked, the ladies proceeded back out into the street. Slowly, they strolled down the busy thoroughfare to where the carriage waited. Avidly, Henrietta drank in the sights of street sellers and pedestrians, shop windows displaying everything from colored prints to china and glass.

Nell's concentration was focused on less frivolous matters. "Those robberies you were telling me about," she said abruptly. "Have there been further developments? Have the thieves been caught?"

Eleanor's question caught Henrietta by surprise. "*What* robberies—oh! I have read no more about it lately—but you may be sure the culprits will not long escape the notice of Bow Street."

"Ah." Lady March hoped she might be sure of no such thing. "*Then* what will happen to them, do you think?"

"What will happen to the thieves, you mean?" It was a queer question, Henrietta thought. "The same thing that usually happens to thieves, I suppose. They will be clapped in prison, there to await their trial."

The ladies had arrived at the carriage, an elegant

cabriolet which sported the family crest. "And after they stand their trial, *then* what?" inquired Eleanor, as she climbed inside.

"Why, then I suppose they will be either transported or hanged." Henrietta settled her bulk on the cotton-upholstered seat. "You are very interested in these robberies, Eleanor!"

Little did Henrietta realize the extent of her interest, Lady March thought grimly. Nor did Eleanor intend she should find out. "Anyone must be concerned. If this menace is permitted to continue unchecked, it will be safe for no one to venture out-of-doors."

With a pleasurable shudder, as if she expected to be momentarily set upon, Henrietta surveyed the street. Discovering no dangerous-looking scoundrels lurking among the pedestrians and street sellers, the porters and ballad singers and clerks, she sank back on her seat. "I make no doubt the rascals will eventually be brought to justice," she said indifferently. "There have been handbills distributed, and reward offered."

Handbills? Reward? With every fresh disclosure, Eleanor grew more apprehensive, until she expected momentarily to be taken into custody herself, in connection with a certain shabby valise currently hid beneath her four-poster bedstead. "I know little of such things," she murmured. "What exactly is *done* to people who break the law?"

Though Henrietta was little better informed, it was not her practice to admit ignorance. She drew on her active imagination, well-fueled by the newssheets. "The most dreadful things, upon my word!" she responded knowledgeably. "You would not believe the half of it!"

"Such as?" Nell prepared to hear the worst.

Henrietta was not long at a loss. "I could not reconcile it with my conscience to speak to you of such improper things," she said piously. Then her glance sharpened. "Why are *you* so curious, by the by? Since you do not wear jewelry, you are not likely to be robbed."

The last thing Lady March wished to do was further rouse Henrietta's suspicions. Already Marriot hesitated to send her packing, lest she sense something in the wind. "Anyone must be curious!" Nell protested. "When you said you had read no more about the robberies lately, did you mean that none have occurred recently, or that you have not been reading the newssheets?"

"I meant that, to the best of my knowledge, no further robberies have occurred for several days." Henrietta would have sooner given up her morning chocolate than her newssheets—this, despite her taste for sweets. What possible reason could Eleanor have for this sudden interest in crime and punishment?

Abruptly, an explanation presented itself. Henrietta's eyes bulged. "Eleanor! You don't think that Marriot—"

"Of course I do not!" Frantic to put off her companion, Eleanor looked—and sounded—very cross. "I beg you will not be such a ninnyhammer, Henrietta! I merely do not care to think I may be murdered in my bed." This unfortunate choice of words prompted her to grimace. "By thieves!"

Henrietta abandoned the intriguing notion of why thieves should thus comport themselves in Lady March's bedchamber for even more intriguing speculation upon what connection thieves might have with the bizarre behavior of Lord March. Or perhaps their involvement was with Lady Amabel, whose conduct had lately been more than strange. That some connection existed, Henrietta was certain. Her instinct for mischief was acute.

Nor was Henrietta distracted by Eleanor's attempts to throw her off the track. "Just why *did* Marriot disappear in that queer manner?" she inquired.

"He did not mean to disappear, precisely." Now it was Lady March who fixed her attention on the street. "We have explained all that. What has Marriot to do with the present conversation? I thought we were talking about thieves. Of course, we are much less likely to fall victim to such villains now that there is again a man in the house! Not that the servants weren't there all along—but you know what I mean!"

"Do not distress yourself, Eleanor!" In point of fact, Henrietta did *not* take Lady March's meaning, nor know what had prompted the distressed look on her patrician face. "I will not press you further for an explanation, even though it's my opinion no one can seriously credit the story you've put about. Cornwall! Poppycock! But that's no bread-and-butter of mine. Just remember, Eleanor, should you wish to *confide* in someone, that my concern must always be *your* best interest!"

"Thank you, Henrietta! You are very good." Only barely did Lady March repress a shudder. Confidences as rendered up to Henrietta would speedily be noised about the town. "I will bear in mind your offer—though I cannot imagine what I would wish to confide in anyone *about!*"

"Can you not?" Henrietta brushed futilely at the wisps of white hair which had escaped from beneath her domed straw bonnet to tickle cheek and brow. "But I am promised to say no more on *that* head!" Once more she glanced out into the street, then frowned. "How odd!"

"*What* is odd?" Eleanor thrust aside a graphic vision of her husband being taken into custody for the possession of stolen goods, and summarily hanged. "What are you looking at?"

Henrietta was looking at a bonnet of red silk trimmed round the front with black velvet and ornamented with a black feather—a bonnet which she fancied she'd seen several times before. Could they be being *followed?* The bonnet was swallowed up in the crush of traffic and pedestrians. "I had thought—but it was just my imagination!" she replied.

CHAPTER TWELVE

While Henrietta imagined that she was being followed by a red silk bonnet trimmed with black velvet and a feather, Amabel was indulging in some imaginative reasoning of her own. "Fergus's ardor has cooled," she said sadly. "It must have done—I never was so snubbed—not that he was all *that* ardent in the first place! Would *you* require that a girl *ask* you to kiss her, Marriot?"

Lord March glanced up from his book. "That would depend upon the young lady," he responded with quirked brow.

Lady Amabel wrinkled her pretty nose, which was a not unbecoming shade of pink. Mab was not looking quite herself, result of having passed a very agitated night, during which visions of Lord Parrington and his mama had paraded incessantly through her head. "You are bamming me," she said. "I know you don't truly want to kiss anyone but Nell. Nor should you! But *did* you wish to do so, even did it land you in the briars, you wouldn't then tell a girl she shouldn't have asked you to in the first place!"

Since further opportunity for a perusal of its pages was to be denied him, Marriot set aside his book. "This young man of yours sounds like a dull stick!" he replied.

"A dull—oh!" Amabel was hurt. "How prodigious unfeeling you are, Marriot! Fergus is no such thing. And if he *is*, it's entirely his mama's fault. I'll tell you what, Marriot: sometimes I wish I'd stayed in the country!"

With this sentiment, Lord March sympathized; sometimes he wished he'd remained safely indoors on a certain fateful evening instead of sallying forth to White's. This opinion he put forth.

"One cannot *blame* Fergus for being prodigious concerned about what his mama may say to him," insisted Mab, as she paced the solar. Mab was this day in perfect harmony with her Elizabethan surroundings, with her round gown of yellow spotted muslin, wearing a tall steeple hat she'd retrieved from the attics, and carrying a lute. "I don't doubt for a moment that the old tartar can kick up a dreadful rowdy-do. If only Fergus had a little more resolution! The next thing I know his mama will have persuaded him to hedge off." She paused by the counting table. *"Bother* the woman! Let us talk of something else."

Lord March, seated on an embroidered chair, stretched out his long legs, clad this day in unmentionables and hessian boots, with which he wore a buff kerseymere waistcoat, and a single-breasted morning coat of olive-green cloth. "Gladly, brat!" he said.

"Am I being a dreadful bore?" Looking rueful, Lady Amabel drew up a studded, velvet-upholstered stool. "I am sorry for it. I am not accustomed to being treated in a cavalier fashion, Marriot—no, or to admirers who blow first hot, then cold." She rubbed her reddened nose. "Not that Fergus was ever other than lukewarm! It will serve me right for putting myself forward, you think. But I do not mean to go boring on about *my* sad fix! I have not forgot that yours is much worse."

Though Marriot had hardly overlooked his problems, Mab's lamentations had allowed him a temporary respite. Now, unhappily, he recalled that he had a veritable quicksand from which to extricate himself, and no means of rescue in sight. "I had expected some indication from *some*one," he admitted. "Apparently I was too optimistic. The only reaction to my return that I have noticed is a great deal of gabble-grinding as to why I went away!"

"Yet someone must know the truth of it." Mab looked enchanting in her tall hat, which was made of the white bark of a lime tree and adorned with fringes and braids and peacock plumes. "What about the person—or people—who hit you over the head? Who may or may not

97

have been the thieves? And what about the thieves themselves, who *must* know you have the jewels?"

"I could well be a thief myself, remember." Lord March reached out for the lute. "We must not discount that possibility—or the possibility that no one knows I *have* the accursed things, although I can't think how that might have come about."

Lord March's thinking, Mab had noticed, went forth much more lucidly when his wife was not in the immediate vicinity. It must be very nice to command such devotion, she thought sadly, recalling Lord Parrington's preoccupation with whether his parent had got the wind up.

But prolonged contemplation of Fergus and his mama would only cast her into despair. "You're not scorched, are you, Marriot? Run aground? Because if you *did* steal those jewels, there must be some reason *why*."

"I thought of that already, brat. My man of business assures me I'm nowhere near the River Tick."

"No? Well then, can you still remember *nothing*, Marriot? All we know is that you came back to us smelling of the stable—which is not of the slightest help in determining where you've *been!* If not for those wretched jewels we might be more open in our inquiries." She shook her head. "If I am in the briars, Marriot, *you* are in a cleft stick!"

Expertly, Lord March handled the lute, which was large and pear shaped with a long neck. "Much as Nell may dislike it, I think our inquiries—or mine, at least—must take a different direction. *Some*one must be looking for me. I must become more accessible."

"Oh, certainly! So that you may be hit over the head once more." Mab was scornful. "You cannot expect someone to walk boldly up and ask what's become of the jewels, Marriot!"

"I suppose not." In point of fact, Lord March had anticipated a development of that sort. He had thought, upon his reappearance, that some noteworthy event would transpire—and so it had, but he could hardly take credit for the disruption of Mab's romance. "Come out of the mops, brat! It is not so bad as all that."

But Lady Amabel's pained expression had been prompted not by her own thoughts, but by the extremely inharmonious sounds issuing from his lordship's lute. The lute, she suspected, had not been tuned since Elizabethan days. "Matters are bad enough!" she said severely. "Don't forget that you share your residence with a prattle-bag. You must be constantly on your guard against your cousin, Marriot! Look what her tale-pitching has cost me! She has cut up all my hopes. In *your* case, much more than your hopes may be cut up—or stretched!"

Lord March's expression was also pained, result not of the discordant notes plucked by his fingers from the lute strings. "Point taken, brat! Perhaps now you will tell me how I may see to it that Henrietta does not inadvertently arrange to have my neck stretched."

"I wish I might!" Mab wrinkled her brow in thought, thus disarranging her conical hat, which she subsequently pulled off. "Perhaps we should ask Nell to arrange a soirée. Then we may watch the people who come into the house, and discover if any of them try to nose out the jewels. *If* anyone knows you have the things, they will doubtless try to get them back." She glanced suspiciously around her. "You may not have to make an effort to discover those who know what you have been up to—they may come to *you!* Have you thought of *that,* Marriot?"

"I have." It had also occurred to Lord March that no sweet and intimate tones issued from his lute. "You need not fear unwelcome guests, Mab. Marcham Towers is a veritable fortress. Are you thinking of the hidden tunnel which runs beneath the gardens? Only I know the entrance."

"I hope you are correct." Lady Amabel did not look entirely convinced.

Marriot set aside his lute, leaned forward, pinched her cheek. "Trust me, brat!" he said.

"Trust you? Oh, I do!" Mab caught and nuzzled his

hand. "My thoughts are not worth the purchase of a guinea, but *you* are not to blame! I cannot help but remember how *cool* Fergus was to me on our last meeting, and how attentive he was to Nell."

"To *Nell?*" Lord March looked astonished at this intimation that his wife had caught another gentleman's eye. "That coxcomb is on the dangle for Nell?" he snapped.

"Fergus is *not* a coxcomb!" Lady Amabel indignantly retorted, and thrust away Lord March's hand. "He is a — a diamond of the first water, and it is not his fault if he is also a teeny bit craven. Anyone would be who was under his mama's thumb." Her blue eyes narrowed. "If Lady Katherine did not approve of me, she will be thrown into the devil of a pucker by the discovery that Fergus has a tendresse for Nell, and it will serve her right! Lady Katherine, that is, not Nell! I'm sure Nell did not *mean* to steal a march on me. Oh, if I had only known how dreadfully it would all turn out, I would never have invited Fergus to kiss me. It isn't wonderful that he should think me shockingly forward."

Lest Amabel fire up at him again, Marriot refrained from expressing his conviction that Lord Parrington was a coxcomb. "Don't go into high fidgets! Just because your beau is on terms of amity with Nell is no cause for despair."

Terms of amity? Marriot was not familiar with the very formal manner in which Fergus paid a lady court. Eleanor would not understand the baron's cool manner either, Mab thought. Not that hope might exist for Fergus even *did* Nell realize that he held her in admiration. Mab could not decide if she felt more chagrined by Fergus's defection, or sorry that he was fated to be rejected in turn. No one who knew Lord and Lady March could doubt that each held the other's heart.

Marriot was looking at her oddly, as if he expected some comment. Since naught would come of Fergus's sudden infatuation, there was no reason to prose on about it, Mab thought. Marriot already had unpleasantness enough on his platter without adding to it. "I am being very foolish! I cannot help but remember that I meant to persuade you to put in a good word with my papa about Fergus—and now you needn't bother, because Fergus doesn't *want* me, and even if he did his mama wouldn't let him *have* me, and I can't think of *how* I might detach him from her apron strings!" Upon this admission, she dissolved into tears.

With a resigned expression, Lord March rose from his chair, drew Lady Amabel up from her stool, and allowed her to sob with abandon all over his olive-green coat. It was not the first such garment that Mab had abused during their lifelong acquaintance.

"What a ninnyhammer I am!" Mab raised her head, the force of her unhappiness temporarily spent. "Raising such a dust about my little difficulties when you have far greater difficulties to face. And we have done nothing to solve *either* of our problems, and soon Henrietta will be home, and we must all practice dissimulation again. It never ceases to amaze me, Marriot, that you can be connected with so *unobliging* a female!"

In his turn, Lord March never ceased to be amazed by Lady Amabel's ability to cry without leaving a trace. If anything, a fit of sobbing left Mab even prettier than before its inception, with bright eyes and delicately flushed cheeks. With a careless finger, he brushed the tears from her cheeks. "Don't despair; we'll think of something, brat. If nothing else, I can insist that you've been compromised. You will recall that I offered to come the heavy with Parrington. Even with your invitation, he should not have kissed you, Mab."

This, from a gentleman positively addicted to kissing his own wife, was a very selfish attitude, Mab thought. "Ah! You never kissed Nell before you were married? Who'd have thought it?" She grinned.

Marriot smiled also. "Perhaps a time or two— touché, brat! However, Nell did not have to ask me, and we were officially betrothed, and consequently there was little harm in it. *This* business is different. You, too, must look sharp about you, Mab. I have warned Henrietta that the direst consequences will

101

descend upon her does she spread *this* tale about, but you must be aware that she holds you in dislike. If your papa hears Parrington has been embracing you beneath my roof, I doubt I can reconcile him with any number of good words."

This aspect of the situation had not previously struck Lady Amabel. Looking very guilty, she caught her lower lip between her teeth. Only the butler's appearance in the doorway prevented her from bursting into dramatic speech.

Accustomed as he was to Mab's histrionics, Marriot did not feel up to another display just then. "In a moment, Benson!" he said to the butler. "Don't go into high fidgets, Mab. We will think of some way out of this coil. Whatever may develop, I won't permit you to be compromised."

This bracing reassurance had not the precise effect his Lordship had anticipated. "Oh, Marriot!" wailed Lady Amabel, and collapsed upon his chest. Wearing a rueful face, Lord March drew her closer and in an avuncular manner stroked her dark curls.

"Come, come, Mab!" he murmured. "What's all this? Did you expect me to leave you to work out your own problems? You *are* under my protection, brat!" Alas for Lord March's good intentions. In light of his own difficulties, Marriot would have been wise to pay closer heed not only to his audience, but also his words.

That audience consisted not only of the superior wooden-faced butler, but the callers who had believed it beneath their dignity to cool their heels in the great hall while their advent was announced. "Aha!" uttered the eldest of these callers in highly vindictive tones. "Under the rogue's protection, is she? Faith, it *is* a slyboots!"

"What the *devil?*" inquired Lord March in almost the same breath.

He did not receive enlightenment just then. Amabel recognized Lady Katherine's undulcet voice. Peering around Marriot's shoulder, she saw Lord Parrington's ashen, horrified face. Clearly the newcomers had
102

gravely misconstrued the scene. One could hardly blame them. Here was a pickle as pretty as any damsel had ever landed in, thought Mab as she gracefully swooned.

CHAPTER THIRTEEN

Returning home from her expedition to Oxford Street, Lady March was met by her butler in the great hall. "Oh, milady!" groaned that haughty individual, in a more emotional state than his mistress had ever witnessed him. "It is the most *dreadful* thing!"

"*What* is dreadful, Benson?" Eleanor was visited by an appalling conviction that during her absence Marriot had been dragged off to Newgate. "Answer me, pray!"

In response, the butler shuddered. "In the solar, milady—" In a disapproving, distinctly ghoulish manner, he explained what had so recently transpired. "Oh, the devil!" muttered Nell.

"I *knew* it!" crowed Henrietta, plump face alight with triumph. "I knew that chit was no better than she should be! Yes, and I warned you not to leave her alone with Marriot, if you will recall. Poor Lady Katherine will be in a taking! I must go to her immediately!"

"You must *not!*" retorted Lady March in such grim tones that Henrietta paused mid-stride. "This business is largely of your making, and I do not intend that you should meddle more."

The butler, who was no fonder of Henrietta than any other member of the household, cleared his throat. "If I may say so as shouldn't, milady, it wasn't my impression that the master and Lady Amabel were—er."

Henrietta roused sufficiently from her mistreatment, the shock of which had caused her to lean against a suit of armor for support, to award the butler a look of keen dislike. "Impertinent! Of course they were."

Wistfully, Lady March eyed the rack of spears set upon the ancient walls. Resolutely she turned and mounted the great staircase with its carved balustrades and newel posts. She did not trust herself to speak to Henrietta.

Meantime, in the solar, Lord March was the target of a great many words, most noteworthy among which to date had been "hussy," "baggage" and "jade," Marriot could not fail to admire Lady Katherine's invective, even while regretting the situation in which he had been placed. In the delivery of verbal levelers, Lady Katherine would have few equals. She was fast on her feet and quick to pop one in over an opponent's guard. Marriot—who in his salad days had been a great deal addicted to sport—thought he would have liked to have the handling of her in the ring.

Currently, Lady Katherine was standing up for a round or two with her own son, with whom it had been bellows to mend after the first onslaught. "I do not think you should call Lady Amabel a trollop, Mama," he persisted, battered but still game. "Nor do I think you should call *me* a loose-screw. In fact, Mama, I wish you would cut line!"

"You wish I would—" Lady Katherine's raddled features turned an ugly mottled shade. "Shall I tell you what *I* wish, you young jackanapes? I wish you had never met this scheming little minx! You were a dutiful and obedient boy until the chit turned your head with her caressing ways. I do not blame you, son! The hussy set her cap at you. See how she appreciates the distinguishing attentions you paid her—by coquetting with March the instant your back is turned! The girl is a complete flirt. But I will not say I told you so!"

Great as was the entertainment he was deriving from Lady Katherine's performance, which was accompanied by alternate waving of walking stick and vinaigrette, Lord March felt compelled to offer a word in his own and Lady Amabel's behalf. "Mab was not coquetting with me," he explained.

Lady Katherine was very displeased by this interruption. "Don't try and spin *me* a Banbury tale!" she snapped. "We *saw* you embracing the chit."

"I was *not* embracing her." Lord March's attention
105

was directed not at Lady Katherine, enthroned on the day bed, nor Lord Parrington, who stood by the fireplace. Instead he spoke to the doorway. "Mab was in a fit of the blue devils, and I was attempting to persuade her to come out of the mops. Although I am devoted to Mab, I would as soon have a bit of frolic with Cousin Henrietta. You will forgive me, I am certain, for being frank!"

Lady Katherine was not of a forgiving nature. "Zounds!" she uttered, and well might have expounded on that statement had not Eleanor intervened.

"*What* a contretemps!" said Nell, as she walked into the room. Ironically, she surveyed Marriot, who still clutched the swooning Amabel. For a moment, as Nell paused in the doorway, she had wondered if Henrietta's dire prophecy had indeed come true. But if Nell couldn't trust Marriot and Mab—it didn't bear thinking about.

"Lady March!" Lord Parrington stepped forward. "I am very sorry that you should have to discover this!"

"Discover what?" Having reached her husband's side, Eleanor gazed up into his face. "Do you still insist that Marriot was embracing Mab? Benson told me all about it, when I encountered him belowstairs. This is a great piece of work about nothing. If I don't mind whether Marriot embraces Mab—and I don't!—why should anybody else?"

"Darling!" Had his arms been free, Lord March would have embraced his wife.

At this point, Lady March would have appreciated an embrace. She frowned at the impediment which stood—or swooned— between her and this relief. His lordship did likewise.

As if in response to this concentrated attention, Lady Amabel opened one blue eye. "Hallo! I'm dashed glad to see you, Nell! Maybe you can convince Lady Katherine that when Marriot said I was under his protection, he meant under his *roof!*"

Lady Katherine, too long overlooked, brandished her walking stick. "Hah!" she barked.

Now that Mab had removed herself from Marriot's

arms, Nell appropriated one of those appendages for her own use. Soberly, she regarded Lady Katherine, who wore a quantity of mohair fabric, and with it a somewhat incongruous bonnet of white muslin tied under the chin. "You have been misled by Henrietta, I conjecture," Nell charitably remarked. "Not that Henrietta would *deliberately* mislead you, but she has a tendency to *over*state the case."

That failing, thought Lord Parrington, Eleanor did not share. He was astonished and touched by her trust. Only the noblest of ladies, greeted by the spectacle of her husband clasping another female, would be put off by so very lame a tale.

"I'll say Henrietta overstates the case!" muttered Lady Amabel, who had withdrawn to the oriel window from which vantage point she had an excellent view of Fergus gazing like a mooncalf at Nell. "I never engaged in a bacchanalian scene in all my life! Or a squalid little debauch! Nor do I intend to do any such thing. But I have noticed that the misdeeds persons accuse you of are most often the ones they would like to commit themselves!"

Everyone was silenced by the suggestion that Henrietta secretly yearned to desport herself in a bacchanalian manner. Lady Katherine elevated her scowling attention from her walking stick, Lord Parrington lowered his gaze from the ceiling, Lord and Lady March ceased to look ruefully upon one another; and all stared astonished at Lady Amabel. Mab shrugged. "This is all fudge!"

"Fudge?" Having caught her breath, Lady Katherine was prepared to go another round. "*Fudge,* is it? Well, *I* for one am glad this happened, miss! We have seen you in your true colors. Scant chance *now* that you may lead my lamb astray."

Though Lord Parrington was out of charity with Lady Amabel, Fergus could not permit his mama to subject her to a rake down. In point of fact, Fergus also felt out of charity with his mama. "You are coming it much too strong, Mama!" he said.

"I am *what?*" Lady Katherine reared back in her chair, horrified. Here was strong proof of Amabel's influence. "Plague on't, I've done no such thing!" she cried, inhaling deeply of her vinaigrette.

"Oh yes, you have!" Mab departed the window and approached Lady Katherine. In so doing, she passed the tall steeple hat which she had worn earlier, retrieved it, and clapped it on her head. "You have kicked up the most dreadful dust over the merest trifle, just like Fergus said you would!"

"Fergus said—" Lady Katherine craned her head to observe her offspring, who was thoughtfully watching Lady March. Lady Katherine could not approve this open admiration of another man's wife. "Young man, explain yourself!"

"Hmmm?" Fergus adjudged, very correctly, that his mama would not care to hear his sentiments concerning Eleanor, whose nobility of character enabled her to calmly accept not only the intelligence that her husband was prone to peccadilloes, but the young lady whom he had been openly intriguing with. Or perhaps it was true, as Mab insisted, that they had been deceived in what they saw. Mab certainly looked a treat in that absurd tall hat, trimmed with fringe and braids and plumes. Fergus smiled.

Nor did Lady Katherine approve her offspring's admiration of the young woman who had so recently, and before their very eyes, been trifled with by another man. "I wish you would tell me," she said sternly, "why you told this chit that I kick up dusts!"

"I don't know why he *shouldn't* have told me," inserted Lady Amabel. "You *do* kick up dusts! You're kicking up one now!"

Lady Katherine's glance would in itself have been sufficient to quell a less dauntless damsel. Lady Amabel met it with pugnaciously outthrust lower lip. Lord Parrington retired to the oriel window, clearly wishing no part of the scene.

At this point, Lord March regretfully unclasped his wife, deeming it time for diversion, before Lady Katherine and Mab resorted to actual fisticuffs. "It is Mab who should be kicking up a dust," he observed. "Since it is *her* reputation that has been compromised."

Lady Katherine did not remove her basilisk stare from Mab's rebellious face. "You compromised the chit; you make reparations!" she snapped.

"Marriot did not compromise Mab!" protested Nell, thus elevating herself even more in Lord Parrington's opinion. Fergus had never before met a female who could confront adversity without becoming indisposed.

"Certainly I did not." Lord March picked up the lute. "I merely sought to comfort her. It was your son, ma'am, who besmirched Mab's good name."

"Gracious!" Lady Amabel turned an amazed look on Marriot. *"Has* my name been besmirched?"

"We must hope it has not—but that depends on Henrietta, and how far she's spread the tale." Lord March strummed a mournful, and most untuneful, chord.

At this suggestion that the better part of London might soon be apprised that Lord Parrington had been caught embracing Lady Amabel, the occupants of the solar all were appalled. Lady March hastened to her husband's side, there to be patted and soothed; Lady Katherine muttered nastily beneath her breath. Lord Parrington, less accustomed to giving vent to his feelings, stared out the window.

Thus granted opportunity to do so without attracting attention, Mab studied him. Fergus looked as correct as usual in light blue merino trousers and a dark brown frock coat—and as handsome to behold.

Mab walked toward him, pulling off the tall hat. "I truly am sorry for all this fuss and botheration," she said. "Let us cry friends, Fergus! You know that what you saw wasn't what it seemed, I think."

Lord Parrington looked down into Amabel's pretty face. He did not *want* to believe he had been so deficient in good judgement as to have favored a damsel prone to run wild over other gentlemen. Still, Mab *had* treated him very coolly, which he could not help but

109

resent, even while admitting she had not lacked provocation. "I don't know what I saw!" he confessed.

Though Lord Parrington might vacillate, his mama possessed no such doubts. "Stab me, but the boy's a clunch!" she remarked to the room at large, as with the assistance of her walking stick she struggled upright. "If her behavior was so innocent, why did the chit have recourse to fainting fits? Misunderstood, is she? Paugh! Depend upon it, things were exactly what they seemed— if not *worse!*"

"Oh!" Mab gazed beseechingly at the baron, her blue eyes filled with tears. "You cannot believe such things of me, Fergus—even though I perfectly comprehend why you do not care to do or say anything that will set up your mama's back!"

Not surprisingly, this statement had precisely that effect. "Baggage!" uttered Lady Katherine, and for emphasis brought her walking stick down sharply on the floor. Unfortunately, her foot was in the way.

"Mama!" protested Lord Parrington, unaware that his parent's outcry was not furious, but pained. "Already too much has been said. Pray do not make a further exhibition of yourself."

"A—" Lady Katherine clenched her teeth against additional vituperations, an act of forebearance that deceived no one, due to her countenance of dreadfully gathering rage. "Consider, son! Is this chit worthy of your championship? Why, when we first called on her, she couldn't even be bothered to put in an appearance."

"Well, I like that!" protested Mab inaccurately. "I didn't even know you were here. Henrietta *might* have informed me of your presence, but did she? Oh, no!"

"Henrietta couldn't have very well informed you, Mab!" pointed out Lady March, determined to be fair. "As I recall, you were in the attics with Marriot."

"With Marriot!" Lady Katherine pounced. "What's this? I thought he was in Cornwall!"

"So I was." Lord March wished that he might duplicate his famous disappearing trick. "Nell has gotten confused. If Mab was in the attics, it must have been with you, puss."

"You are correct, of course!" Eleanor blushed. "I can't imagine what I was thinking about!"

If Nell lacked acquaintance with her thoughts, few other occupants of the solar were similarly unblessed. The better to pursue those thoughts—to the secret relief of all those occupants—Marriot set aside his lute. Before he begged his wife to speak her mind, he must ensure their privacy. "Which brings us back to the inescapable fact that Mab's good name has been besmirched."

"Quiet, Mama!" Lord Parrington saw his duty clear—he could hardly fail to do so, so frequently had it been pointed out. "There is but one honorable resolution. I know you will not like it, but Lady Amabel and I must wed."

"*She* will not like it?" So very indignant was Mab's tone and demeanor—blue eyes ablaze, fists on her plump muslin-covered hips—that Fergus fell back a pace. "Your *mama* will not like it? I shall tell you something, Fergus: neither would *I!*"

By this abrupt volte-face, Lord Parrington was confused. "But, Mab, you said—"

"The devil with what I said!" Lady Amabel stamped her own pretty little foot, without adverse result. "Whatever I said, it was before I realized that you *are* a dull stick! And a popinjay, just as Papa said!"

"A *dull stick?*" Lord Parrington was saved from the disgrace of descending to an exchange of insults by the reappearance of the butler.

"Milady," said that haughty individual, whose impassivity had begun to fray, "there is A Person desirous of speaking with you downstairs."

CHAPTER FOURTEEN

Henrietta paced the solar, from the great staircase to the carved and wainscoted screen. Throughout these perambulations, her keen gaze remained fixed on the caller, a nondescript female in a shabby black pelisse. With that pelisse, the woman wore a red silk bonnet trimmed with black velvet and a feather. As result of that red silk bonnet, Henrietta's vast instinct for mischief was hard at work. "You have been following us!" she observed.

The shabby individual dropped an awkward curtsey. "That I have, mum. I was wishful of speaking to Lady March. In fact, since you tell me you ain't her ladyship—not that I thought you was—I still *am!*"

This frank hint reminded Henrietta that since Benson had already gone to fetch Eleanor, her own time was short. Determined to make the most of her opportunity, she approached the stranger. "You cannot simply walk into a house and demand to see its mistress, my good woman! What did you wish to speak to Lady March about?"

"I'll tell her ladyship that!" responded the visitor, looking stubborn. "'Tis personal-like!"

On closer inspection, discovered Henrietta, the woman was no less nondescript. Everything about her lacked definition—hair, complexion, figure, eyes. She was the sort of person who would blend perfectly with any crowd. "What is your name?" Henrietta inquired.

Again that awkward curtsey, which may have been meant to mock. "Jane Verney, mum," the stranger replied.

"How d'ye do, Jane?" Henrietta was not adverse to hobnobbing with the lower orders—for the sake of good gossip, Henrietta would probably have been willing to rub shoulders with the Great Fiend himself. What reason could such a creature have for seeking out Eleanor? she again asked silently. Then she sat smack down on a chest carved in a checkered pattern. "Marriot!" she gasped.

The visitor looked cautious. "Beg pardon, mum?"

"You need not come the innocent with me, my girl!" Hot on the scent of scandal, Henrietta was even more anxious to learn all she could before Eleanor's arrival set her interrogation awry. "You are here because of Marriot. The rogue! To think that a relative of mine—the shame of it! I told Eleanor what would happen—not that I knew about *you*—but I *did* know she shouldn't trust him one inch!"

To these observations, the visitor responded with discretion. "Lawks!" she said.

Here was scandal enough to satisfy anyone, thought Henrietta; a pity she was under obligation to protect the family name. Now she must hasten to discover the precise nature of the scandal before Eleanor intervened. "I *knew* he wasn't in Cornwall!" she muttered. "Or *was* he? You can tell me that, I'll wager! Speak up, miss!"

Jane Verney was no such obliging creature. "I'm sure I don't know what you're talking about, mum!"

"And you don't know either why Marriot and Eleanor quarreled?" Henrietta shifted on the wooden chest, which made no comfortable seat even for a lady so well-supplied with flesh. "Poppycock! Do not try and gammon me. Anyone must see you are here because of Marriot."

As it turns out, Jane was indeed come to Marcham Towers in regard to its master, a fact she was not disposed to point out. "Is that so?" she inquired.

"You know it is." Henrietta glanced at the great staircase, upon which Eleanor had not yet appeared. Hopefully, Lady Katherine's vaporing would keep Nell safely abovestairs. "Let us have the word with no bark on it! I *might* be useful to you, you know—were you to confide in me, I might help you present your case."

"Useful, mum?" This suggestion sparked a gleam in Jane's pale eye. "How's that?"

"You are a stranger. My word, as a member of the family, will carry more weight." That she was the least favored of the family, Henrietta didn't feel obligated to confide. "We are wasting time! Come, tell me what you know of Marriot."

"It don't seem right, mum. To be talking about a person behind his back." Jane did not deem it politic to admit how very little she knew of Lord March. "But if you say I should—"

"I do say it! Did he tell you *not* to speak of him? You must not regard that!" Henrietta coaxed.

Jane's pale glance moved around the great hall, flickered over racks of spears and suits of armor, lowered to the marble chessboard floor. "He didn't exactly *say* I should be as close as oysters!" she muttered with perfect truth.

Here was progress! "What *did* he say?" Henrietta leaned forward, intent.

Jane did not feel qualified to answer that question, not knowing what answer would best suit her purposes—which, for the record, were not of pure intent. "I can't tell you that, mum. It ain't my place."

"You may tell me at least if you made Marriot's acquaintance during the last six months." As did any good talebearer, Henrietta had it in her to be sly. "Yes? And I'll wager you didn't meet him in Cornwall. I thought not! Which means that Marriot was never *in* Cornwall! I knew it! I knew mischief was afoot." The nature of that mischief still eluded her, however. She frowned. What could this nondescript female have to do with Marriot? Only one explanation presented itself. Henrietta's scowl turned to a look of astonishment. What appeal would this pale creature have for a man married to Nell? For that matter, what appeal had Lord Parrington for Eleanor, and Marriot for Lady Amabel? Clearly there was no logic to matters of the heart. "Poor thing!" she said sympathetically. "You don't *look* like—well!"

114

"That's because I ain't!" Jane had a strong sense of preservation, and an equally well-developed sense of expediency, and she instinctively understood which rôle would be most advantageously enacted. "I had me a nice little job in a shop—before himself led me astray. At home to a peg he was! Or so I thought—though I ain't sure but what I'd've thought differently had I suspected how things would fall out!"

"How *did* things fall out?" Fascinated, Henrietta stared.

"Turrible!" Jane revealed none of the truimph she felt as result of the ease with which her quarry had risen to her bait. "I thought himself had stuck his spoon in the wall. Not that I ain't glad to discover he *hasn't*— I didn't know he *was*, you ken! Which just goes to show that a girl *shouldn't* allow herself to be stood to a glass of flesh and blood by a well-breeched swell!"

So very excited was Henrietta rendered by these disclosures that she rose up off the chest. "You poor, *poor* thing!" she cried. "You discovered that the man who'd led you astray and then abandoned you—he *did* abandon you? I thought he must have!—was not only still alive, but had returned to his home. And so you followed him, in hope of—" Henrietta looked blank. "In hope of what?"

Jane's aspirations were best kept private. Therefore she said nothing, but sat down on the chest. "You wished to see him again!" decided Henrietta, whose suspicious nature and passion for scandal did not preclude a perverse appreciation of romance. "To gaze upon the scroundrel who abandoned you—how sad! But you should not have come here. Marriot will not thank you for it. No gentleman likes to see his dirty linen washed in public—I do not mean to compare *you* to dirty linen, of course—but you *did* ask for Eleanor!"

"I'd've had to be a perfect block to ask for himself!" retorted Jane, who was as shrewd as she was nondescript, and unsentimental to boot.

"You said he stood you to a glass of flesh and blood." Inspiration smote Henrietta. "Was he *foxed?*"

Jane was not unaware of his lordship's tendency toward eccentricity when under the influence of the grape. "Drunk as a wheelbarrow!" she confessed.

"Drunk as—" Henrietta was so moved by this admission that she leaned against a suit of armor for support. "You don't say!"

Nor was Jane entirely unacquainted with Lord March's errant memory, and from various recent statements had concluded very rightly that Marriot himself wasn't certain about his recent activities. For several moments she'd been pondering whether this surprising development might be used to good advantage—or whether it was an example of her recent bad luck. "On the square!" she added solemnly. "Himself had been set upon by footpads when I came across him—aye, and he *would*'ve turned up his toes hadn't I happened along just then. Proper grateful he was to me, too."

"Oh!" Henrietta clutched the suit of armor tighter. "And then?"

Jane looked down at her shoes, which peeped out from beneath her shabby skirts. "Then I took him home, mum! He claimed he didn't know who he was—proper knocked about on the head he'd been! At first I thought he was having me on, but then I twigged he wasn't. The poor bloke couldn't recall a thing afore he was set upon."

Henrietta was very melancholy to think of her cousin in such straits, and fascinated too. "Heavens!" she breathed.

"It was a right rare puzzle!" A covert glance through pale lashes assured Jane that she held her audience enthralled. Here was a flat! she thought. Were more of the nobs so gullible—but alas, they were not. "We rubbed on well enough, and then one day himself just disappeared. Very queer I thought it, the way he sloped off. Then I heard about this missing lordship who'd suddenly come home."

"And you realized that you'd snatched a gentleman back from the jaws of death!" Greatly moved, Henrietta clasped her hands to her breast. "How touching! And how very inconsiderate of Marriot to have nothing more

116

to do with you. Not that it would be proper if he *did,*" she added, belatedly recalling Marriot's wife. "Still, he must be grateful to you for saving his life."

With this latter statement, Jane perfectly agreed. "The way I reckon it is that now he's remembered who he is, he's forgot *me.*"

"How wonderful this is!" Henrietta was rendered almost sunny tempered by this astounding account of her cousin's bizarre conduct and erratic memory. "You would have had no notion of who Marriot was, not being able to read the newspaper accounts—and I'm sure there is no good reason why you should have connected the events! Then you found yourself abandoned! Deserted, cast off! And *then* discovered not only Marriot's identity but his address. In hopes of seeing him again, you followed us home." It occurred to Henrietta that there were several large gaps in this otherwise highly satisfying tale. "Why did you ask for *Lady* March?" she repeated.

"What'd be the point of asking for *Lord* March if himself has forgot me?" Wearying of the uncomfortable checkered chest, Jane removed herself from it and strolled to the far end of the hall, there to peer curiously at the screen of carved and wainscoted wood.

"That is true." Henrietta followed quickly in the stranger's wake. "You still have not explained what you seek with Eleanor. I do not think Marriot will be pleased—remember you or no!—if you acquaint her with this tale."

That Jane didn't give a fig for Lord March's pleasure, she was too sly to remark. "What's a poor girl to do?" she lamented. "When she hasn't a mag with which to bless herself? That's a ha'penny to you, mum! No, and not enough of the Ready-and-Rhino to fetch some panis and cash—bread and cheese!"

"One moment, miss." Henrietta's suspicions reasserted themselves. "Have you come here because you are *impoverished?*"

"Regularly under the hatches, mum! Rolled up!" Aware that her strategy had erred, Jane put on a servile face. "I thought her ladyship might put me in the way of some honest work."

This response was not what Henrietta had expected. "Honest work?" she echoed, blankly.

"Why *not* honest work, mum?" Jane was indignant. "I ain't ready for the other yet! The way I see it, someone owes me *something* for having saved himself from coming by his just deserts. I wouldn't *be* without a feather to fly with if it wasn't for that. I figured the worst her ladyship could do was send me to the right-about, so I decided to put it to the touch."

"I see," murmured Henrietta. In point of fact, Henrietta saw rather more than Jane suspected, including that she was being spun an exceedingly tall tale. The purposes for this deception, Henrietta could not fathom, being unaware that a great many people might have excellent reason for trying to get close to Lord March.

Jane stole another covert glance. Had she retrieved her earlier blunder, or further erred? In case sympathy for her plight had not yet been engendered, she gave vent to a great sigh. Henrietta's attention thus attracted, Jane looked dejected. "It was a crackbrained notion. I shouldn't have come here. But you can't blame a girl for trying *not* to become Haymarket-ware!"

"Certainly not!" agreed Henrietta, although she was uncertain what Haymarket-ware *was*. "What kind of honest work had you in mind?"

"Anything at all, mum." Jane's vagueness is easily explained by the circumstance that she had never done an honest day's work in all her life. "I fancy I can do anything I set my mind to—I ain't proud!"

Proud the creature might not be; Henrietta was willing to wager she lacked equal acquaintance with the truth. About what that truth might be, Henrietta grew very curious. That this vulgar female knew the details of Marriot's mysterious disappearance, Henrietta no longer had any doubt. Yet how to worm those details out of her? "It might be possible," said Henrietta, "to find you a temporary position in this very house."

"In *this* house, mum?" Here was luck better than

any for which Jane had a right to hope. Covetously, she peered around the hall. "Cor! This is something like! I ain't never seen anything so fine."

"I doubt it not." Henrietta resolutely pushed aside her various reservations concerning the scheme. If anyone was to ferret out the truth of Marriot's recent activities, it would have to be herself. Anathema, the thought that the truth might never be known. "You will have to remember your place, miss! I daresay it will not take Eleanor long to find you something suitable."

Jane was sure of it. Were she in Lady March's place, it would not have taken Jane two shakes of a lamb's hindquarters to show herself the door. "Crikey! Herself must be a very fine lady, to bother with the likes of me. Maybe I could do something to repay her kindness. Look after her gowns, for instance. Or her jewels."

Though Henrietta was demonstrably a pigeon for the plucking, she was not so very featherheaded as to grant a stranger access to Eleanor's boudoir. "Lady March does not care for jewelry," she said absently, thereby convincing Jane that her ladyship was queer in the cockloft. "And she already has an abigail. I must think what story we should tell."

"Whatever you say, mum!" Jane responded readily. After all, few dyed-in-the-wool villainesses hold veracity in high repute.

Came Eleanor's voice from the bottom of the great staircase, which she had descended unnoticed: "Tell whom about what, pray?"

"Eleanor!" Henrietta clutched at her throat, then realized Nell could not have overheard a conversation at this end of the hall. What tale would best serve? wondered Henrietta again, as Eleanor approached. The truth? Or some less shocking explanation for the presence of this nondescript female? Jane Verney was a very strange sort of fallen woman in Henrietta's opinion; but she had very little practical knowledge of demireps. One did not expect bits o' muslin to be so very *ordinary,* somehow, or prim—

119

But here was Eleanor come to them, looking weary; and Henrietta must decide. Should she be kind and cushion the blow of Marriot's infidelity—or reveal which one of them knew what was what? Had not Henrietta predicted Marriot was prone to petticoat fever? Had not Eleanor in turn intimated that Henrietta had windmills in her head?

Given this choice, the outcome was never in real doubt. Melodramatically, Henrietta flung her arms wide, in the process knocking Jane's red silk bonnet askew. Eleanor looked startled. Jane neither flinched nor elevated her gaze from her toes.

Well did Henrietta savor this triumphant moment. "*Here* is what Marriot has been up to!" she exclaimed.

CHAPTER FIFTEEN

"There's something damned smokey here!" exclaimed Lord March from the depths of the intricately carved four-poster bedstead, a comment inspired not by his surroundings, but by the story his wife told. "I want to see this female I supposedly seduced."

"No, you do not!" Lady March prevented her husband's hasty departure from the four-poster by grasping the sleeve of his night shirt, an item of masculine attire in which he looked extremely fetching. "Take my word for it! Beside, you have not yet heard the half of what she had to say."

Because his wife looked fetching also in a profusion of cambric muslin and green ribbons, his lordship settled back down by her side. He had not made the acquaintance of this Jane Verney who claimed to know him, having been occupied during that interval with Lady Katherine, who felt that she was supremely meritorious of everyone's attention, as result of her various afflictions—and in the process acted like a very dire affliction herself. Only now, a considerable time later, was he learning what had transpired elsewhere.

Those events Marriot regretted. "You had better tell me all about it!" he said.

Nell did not do so immediately, but smiled at her husband over the rim of her wineglass, the mate to which he held. A fire blazed merrily in the fireplace, glinted off the decorative colored marble, cast merry shadows on the figures and foliage painted on the plaster walls. All in all, it made a cozy domestic scene—amazingly so in view of the recent disclosure that one participant in this snug domesticity had strayed.

Perhaps Nell did not believe the worst of him? "I do

not think I would be unfaithful to you even if I *had* forgot your existence, puss!" said Marriot.

"My darling!" murmured Nell.

Followed an interval during which the wineglasses were emptied, and the fire burned low, and Lord March's nightshirt joined his brocade robe on the floor. "But I must tell you what the creature said!" Lady March remarked at last. "'Tis the most diverting tale. You are at home to a peg, did you know? A very well-breeched swell."

Lord March was not breeched at all in that moment, as became apparent when he reached to retrieve his wineglass. Modestly, if a trifle tardily, her ladyship looked elsewhere. "You were set upon by footpads, and our Jane happened along just in time to prevent you sticking your spoon in the wall, after which she took you along home with her, and proper grateful you were!" Nell paused to accept her replenished wineglass. "I do not know if this was *before* you stood her to a glass of flesh and blood, or *after*—did I say you were in your altitudes? Well, you were! And she lost the nice little job she had in a shop before you led her astray—but neither of you knew who you were because the footpads had knocked you on your head!"

His lordship then offered to perform the same service for Jane. "Ungrateful!" responded Eleanor, whose mood was very frivolous as result of her husband's skilled attentions, and the wine, and the combined events of a long and trying day. "You have already abandoned the wench! *Not* that she holds it against you, mind! She merely wants to be put in the way of a little honest work, since you have left her destitute."

"Nell." Lord March was encouraged by his wife's cheerful demeanor to caress her cheek. "Can this be true?"

"Gudgeon!" Lady March kissed her husband's caressing hand. "If you ever turned an eye of love on that platter-faced female, I'll eat her red silk bonnet!"

Red silk bonnet? A vague memory twinged. Something to do with black velvet trimming and a feather—

but it was all so ephemeral. Yet the creature *had* known about his undependable memory…In an effort to aid his concentration, Marriot retied his wife's green ribbons. "You relieve me, puss! I would not like to think I had fallen into licentious ways."

"Even if you had, it would not signify." Giggling, Eleanor held out her glass. "You were drunk as a wheelbarrow, you will recall. Rather, you *don't* recall, but Jane assures me it is true. When she discovered you had hopped the twig, she was ready to blow her brains out—but then she decided no gentleman was worth putting a period to her existence over, even if he *did* have the others beaten to flinders, which she assures me is the case!"

Eleanor was very calm for a lady whose husband's behavior left much to be desired, thought Marriot. He hoped this fine tolerance was result of believing this odd tale had been made up out of whole cloth. "Did you mean it when you said you didn't *mind* me kissing Mab?" he asked.

"Mind? Why should I?" When her wineglass remained empty, Nell tossed it carelessly aside. It landed uninjured atop her spouse's discarded nightware. Marriot's lugubrious expression struck her. "Oh! You cannot *truly* think I do not mind! That is, I *don't*, but if I thought you really *meant* it, I would mind dreadfully! You cannot expect that I am jealous of Mab, who is our friend—and this Verney female is obviously playing a May-game!"

"I am glad to hear it." In demonstration of this sentiment, Lord March drew his wife down against his chest. "I could never forgive myself if any action of mine—whether in or out of my senses—made you unhappy, Nell!"

"Oh, Marriot!" Lady March snuggled closer. "As if any action of yours *could!*" As result of this exchange, the fire burned lower yet.

"But we must be practical!" decreed her ladyship as she struggled to a sitting position and drew up the ancient fur cloak—which had by now become an integral part of the bed furnishings—over her knees. "I wonder what fish this Jane thinks she may fry—yes, and I wonder also why Henrietta was so quick to insist I help the girl, because I'm quite prepared to wager Henrietta believed her no more than I!" Nell frowned at her spouse. "I just thought of something. Sight of Jane may jog your memory, Marriot."

"Perhaps." In this moment, Lord March aspired toward no sight other than his disarmingly disheveled and somewhat tipsy wife. "And perhaps not! I do not mean to dash your hopes, but it is possible the wench is a stranger, puss. Tell me what she looks like."

"She is—" With a surprised expression, Nell broke off. "I cannot, other than to say she is a very ordinary seeming female. Pale hair and eyes and skin—unexceptional in every way. Also very common! She has a rough, colloquial way of expressing herself."

Lord March reflected silently upon his own recent development of picturesque turns of phrase. "She doesn't sound like a paphian girl."

"I don't think she is." Lady March's uncertainty was due to her lack of intimate acquaintance with such. "Let us say instead that she enjoys freedom from the shackles which hamper a lady of quality. And she tells the most stupendous rappers! I wonder if it has occurred to Henrietta that we may all be murdered in our sleep."

If this possibility had presented itself to Henrietta, it had not done so to his lordship, who as a result sat so abruptly upright that he very nearly tumbled his wife right out of bed. "Calm yourself, Marriot!" she gasped, clutching him. "I charged Benson to keep a sharp eye on our guest! If it *is* the jewels she's after, we need not fear she'll find them, because they are still hidden beneath the bed!"

"You *are* a clever puss!" Marriot settled back amid the pillows, his expression wry. "It is this curst inactivity which has left me on edge."

Because she was a lady, Eleanor made no comment regarding certain very active moments recently shared. And because he knew his wife so well, Marriot guessed

124

her thoughts, even though she said not a word. "Jade!" he murmured, and tweaked a dangling lock. "You take my meaning. We have been waiting for some suspicious move. Finally, things have begun to happen, and I am glad of it."

"Personally, I would welcome a French invasion more!" exclaimed Lady March. "How *can* you talk of inactivity, what with Mab asking Parrington to kiss her and then calling him a dull stick, and being compromised by you and Fergus in turn, and Lady Katherine vaporing, and Henrietta acting the part of a spy—"

Lord March gave the dangling lock a harder tweak. "—and Parrington admiring *you!*" he said.

"Parrington?" Eleanor looked astonished. *"Does* he, do you think?"

From the shadows beyond the embroidered bedhangings came another voice. "Yes, he does!" Holding the Toledo walking sword pugnaciously before her, Lady Amabel approached the bed. "I don't blame you for it, Nell—or him! All the same, it is *me* Fergus wants to marry, and so I mean for him to discover, once this wretched business is cleared up."

Lady March regained her breath, possession of which had temporarily deserted her upon her friend's abrupt appearance. "Mab! You gave me a very nasty turn!" Added Lord March, sternly: "How long have you been here, brat?"

"Long enough!" Mab caught sight of the clothing thrown on the floor. "But not *that* long!" she hastily amended, and discreetly turned her back so that his lordship might retrieve his nightshirt.

With a somewhat wistful expression, Lady March watched her husband perform this act. "You *do* want to marry Parrington, Mab? But you called him a dull stick!"

"And so he is sometimes. What has that to do with it?" Having snatched her ladyship's wineglass off the pile of discarded clothing, Mab refilled it and took a sip.

"You may turn around now, brat," invited Lord March, his rerobing complete. "*And* you may tell us what the devil has brought you here at so advanced an hour, when one might more reasonably expect you to be asleep."

"One might *expect* it, certainly!" Lady Amabel, with wineglass and walking sword, joined Lord and Lady March on the old bed. "One might also be very much mistaken! Has it not occurred to you that if I can just walk into your bedchamber, so might anyone else? And that it is foolish to leave your door unlocked with a strange—and very suspicious!—person in the house? You need not bestir yourself; I locked it behind me, Marriot!" The fire having burned low, the room was cold, and Mab was clad in nothing stouter than her spotted muslin gown. She snuggled under the other end of the ancient fur cloak.

Carefully, Lord March repositioned the Toledo sword, so that it posed less imminent peril to life and limb. "In what manner am I mistaken, brat? Beside yourself, who is not abed?"

Mab chuckled. "You should rather ask who *is!* I see the pair of you are on good terms. Then you aren't angry with Marriot for hugging me, Nell? I am glad of that! I don't think I could bear it if *you* were out of patience with me."

Blushing, Lady March snatched back the hand with which she'd been absentmindedly fondling her husband's knee. "Don't be absurd, Mab!"

"Absurd, am I?" Mab drained her glass. "After the rappers that Verney female has been telling, it wouldn't be wonderful if you *were* feeling a trifle cross! Myself, I've never heard anything half so absurd. She must be very desperate to take so dangerous a gamble, because she could not have known how you would react to her fibs. You might as easily have arranged for her to shelter in gaol as admit her to the house."

"Not really." Lady March rearranged herself, elbows propped on her own knees. "Not without taking the chance that this odious story might get around. The

126

family has already been the focus of more than enough tittle-tattle of late."

"Have you considered that her claims might in some part be true?" Lady Amabel cast Lord March a speculative sideways glance. "Maybe the creature merely wants to be bought off."

"Poppycock!" uttered Nell.

Inserted Marriot, "I am waiting to be enlightened as to who else is abroad at this hour!"

Lady Amabel smiled. "Just about everyone, I think! Benson is trailing the Verney female all about the house. I came very near to skewering Benson on my walking sword before I realized what he was about—and then was almost caught by Henrietta, because she was trailing him! It is really infinitely droll. Benson seemed to be enjoying himself hugely, though Henrietta looked fit to leap out of her skin. I wish she might! And I hope they don't stumble across anything!"

"They won't." Lord March deduced from his wife's awkward posture that she would benefit from a back rub, and immediately embarked upon same. "Unless they also happen upon this chamber. The gems are still hidden under the bed."

On the verge of protesting this poor hiding place, Lady Amabel paused; few safer spots in fact existed than the ancient four-poster, due to the amount of time Lord and Lady March spent therein. "We must not allow ourselves to be thrown into a pucker!" Mab added ironically, her companions having become engrossed in Lord March's ministrations to Lady March's person. "Though I do not believe the Verney woman's story, she must know *some*thing, or she would not have come here at all."

Thus reminded of his peril, Marriot moved away from his wife and idly picked up the walking sword. "We must remember that she asked for *me*," Nell remarked. "I wonder why."

"We must remember also that she seems to have some acquaintance with Marriot's forgetfulness." Disliking his lordship's morose expression, and his fero-

127

cious manipulation of the sword, Mab scooted hastily aside. "She *did* confirm that he'd been set upon by footpads."

"That's not all she confirmed," gloomily uttered Lady March. She could not bring herself to believe that Jane Verney's accusations were true, that Marriot was immensely susceptible to feminine attraction—but how she wished they were well out of this business! And wondered if ever they would be.

"Do you wish me to the devil, my darling?" Become aware that the ladies huddled together on the opposite side of the bed, Marriot threw down the sword. "I could not blame you for it if you did."

"Marriot! Never!" Horrified, Lady March reached out.

"Darling!" responded his lordship, doing likewise.

"Fudge!" interjected Lady Amabel, as between the doting couple she placed the fur cloak and herself. *"Must* the pair of you try and put me to the blush? Or do you simply not care that there are stolen jewels beneath the bed, and a strange woman sneaking about the house, and a very real possibility that Marriot may be hanged? You aren't in your altitudes *now,* are you, Marriot? Then I beg you will try and concentrate your mind!"

"Hanged?" Reminded of this dire possibility, Lady March clutched at her throat. "Mab, how can you say such a thing?"

*"I'*m not the one who wishes to hang him!" True love could be a little tiresome for other than the participants, reflected Lady Amabel. "We do not know that anyone does—or should! In fact, we know precious little, in case you have forgotten, about what Marriot's done or where he's been. Jane Verney is our first real opportunity to find out."

Certain things might be better *not* revealed, mused Eleanor, unaware that her husband's reflections proceeded along similar lines. "How do you propose we make this great discovery? Thus far the woman has told us a tissue of lies."

"Not altogether." Mab nibbled at her lower lip. "We know she's looking for the jewels. And we do not want her to abandon her search, or we will never discover the truth."

Marriot elevated a brow. "Are you suggesting we *give* her the accursed things, brat? If so, I must tell you that though I am concentrating my mind *very* hard, I don't see the use of that!"

"Not give her them, exactly." Mab thought very hard. "We don't want her to get the wind up and smell a rat! But I think we must allow her to guess that we have the jewels, and perhaps even to believe she may get them back."

"A tall order, surely?" Lady March mistrusted her friend's ruminative expression. "How do you think you may bring it off?"

Lady Amabel was triumphant. "With *your* help, very easily, Nell!"

CHAPTER SIXTEEN

Came the eve of Lady March's soirée. All the fashionable world was present, including Lord Parrington, despite his mama's strongly expressed desire that he should not. Fergus had not openly defied his parent, exactly. Instead he left her with the impression that he would gather with convivial souls for dinner and play at Brooke's, as a result of which deception he was feeling very dissatisfied with himself.

That any of his fellow revelers shared his mixed feelings was unlikely, Fergus thought. On this first occasion that Marcham Towers had been thrown open to the public since its master's dramatic reappearance, the old house was crowded with the chosen and the best. Glimpsing his hostess, Fergus made his way toward her through the crush.

Though Lord Parrington might not appreciate the magnitude of this occasion, others were less inclined to nitpick—and even Fergus had to admire the chamber he was in. The long gallery had eleven windows, three of them bays, along its outside wall; and along the inner were two fireplaces, each rectangular, with a chimneybreast rising in three tiers. Near one of those fireplaces stood Lady March. Fergus approached her, a feat not accomplished without the judicious application of his elbow to those persons of the first consideration rash enough to put themselves in his way.

"Hallo, Lady March!" he uttered when he reached her side. To his surprise, she gasped and turned pale.

"Oh, it's you!" Nell said, somewhat inanely, and made a visible effort to collect herself. "Thank goodness! I mean—you took me by surprise!"

Why Lady March should be surprised to be addressed

in a roomful of people, Fergus couldn't guess. "You *did* invite me!" he stiffly pointed out.

"So I did! I did not mean I hadn't!" Eleanor toyed with her necklace, an enormous diamond cut as a rose, in a simple gold setting with a hanging pearl. In point of fact, decided Fergus, Lady March was wearing a prodigious amount of jewelry this evening, including a heavy gold chain set with pearls, a parure of pearls of immense size and beauty, a diamond and gold breast ornament in the form of a bouquet of flowers, and a bracelet with diamonds and emeralds and rubies set in enameled gold. Though Fergus was not so ill-bred as to criticize his hostess, he did reflect that he had not suspected her of having such gaudy taste.

"Oh, dear!" added Eleanor, with her irresistible crooked smile. "I do sound like a zany! Pray forgive me! Things have been at sixes and sevens for so long—and perhaps I need not tell you that Henrietta has been no help! But where is Lady Katherine? Did she not accompany you?"

"I regret that she did not." Surely the baron need not be condemned for this little fib. "I must render my mother's regrets. The, er, exigencies of city life have been too much for her. She is temporarily indisposed."

"I am sorry to hear it," fibbed Nell in turn. At least she need not add worry that Lady Katherine would make a scene to her fear of momentary exposure by the angry owners of the stolen jewelry with which she was draped. Mab's theory was that if sight of the jewels didn't goad Jane to action, they might spark a telling reaction from someone else.

How Jane was to observe the jewels, Mab had failed to explain; the creature would hardly dare push into the long gallery, though she was still in the house, it having been discovered she could sew a tidy seam. As for otherwise smoking out the culprits—Privately, Nell doubted she would recognize a guilty reaction if it took place under her very nose. But better she should run the risk of disclosure than Marriot. Doubtfully, she surveyed her guests, wondering if any among them knew more about Marriot's recent activities than she did, or had hit him on the head. Not until Lord Parrington cleared his throat did Lady March realize that she was guilty of neglect.

"I am so sorry!" Nell clasped her hands tightly together. "*What* you must think of me! I was going over the supper menu in my mind, and hoping the cook has got it right. But I know you will not want to hear such stuff!" She gazed helplessly about, but could see no more than a few feet, so thick was the crowd. "Doubtless you would like to speak with Mab."

Lord Parrington was not certain what he wished to do with Lady Amabel, but among the various possibilities he had recently considered was nothing so mundane as speech. "Perhaps later," he responded. "For the moment, Lady March, I am quite content to converse with *you*."

With *her?* Nell—all this time nodding and smiling and exchanging words of greeting with her other guests—wondered what prompted the baron's odd remark. Then she recalled that Lord Parrington was thought to admire her. Covertly, she regarded him. Very fine he looked in evening breeches and striped silk stockings, exquisite cravat, frilled shirt with high points, white waistcoat, blue coat with very long tails. "Oh!" said she.

That Lady March was no brilliant conversationalist, Fergus had already realized. Perhaps when she was less on the fidgets she had more to say. But why *was* she on the fidgets? Lady March had yet to put forth a reasonable explanation. Was this the behavior of a female whose spouse's conduct was above reproach? Could Eleanor's nonchalance be a sham?

Though Nell did not especially wish to speak with Fergus—or anyone!—she thought she must. Perhaps hope yet remained for the happy outcome of Mab's romance. If only Mab could refrain from being caught out in compromising positions! "I fear Mab is sometimes a little impulsive! Even her papa will agree with me, I think—although it is his fault for having kept her on so loose a rein! You must not hold Mab's high spirits against her, Lord Parrington. I am presumptuous, I know, but Mab is a very good girl."

Fergus had little desire to speak of Mab, whom he'd just glimpsed in animated conversation with Lord March. "I am sure you must have a better idea of what Lady Amabel is and isn't than I!" he responded coolly. "I do not think it would be ungallant in me to say her manners are not what I can *like*."

Nell eyed the baron. Here was starch! Still, if Mab wanted a young man so very high in the instep—"You are feeling a little out-of-sorts," she concluded, "because Mab called you a dull stick! But you had just finished saying you would marry her from a sense of duty, and no young lady likes to hear *that!* Perhaps if you were to try and be a little more romantic—"

Nor did young gentlemen care to hear they were inexpert in matters of the heart. "Hah!" Fergus snapped. "It's hard to be romantic when you've just seen the young lady you're being romantic *about* hugging another man!"

"Hugging—oh, you mean Marriot!" This exchange was proving so engrossing that Eleanor temporarily forgot she was decked out in stolen gems. "That doesn't signify! Mab is just the sort of miss that people *do* wish to embrace!"

Though Fergus might admire his companion's lack of jealousy, he did not aspire to such himself. "I applaud your forebearance, ma'am," he said sincerely. Lady March was convinced her husband harbored no improper feelings toward Amabel, and Fergus could hardly insist otherwise. He sought for diplomacy. "A person doesn't always know when another person is less than he should be."

Lord Parrington now spoke in riddles? So that other among her guests might not be tempted to try and solve his puzzles, Eleanor drew Fergus back beside a draw table, the top of which was inlaid with Elizabethan musical instruments and pieces of music worked in various woods. "Surely what a person may be cannot be so bad as all *that!*" she soothed, under the impression that the baron still smarted under Mab's description of him as a dull stick.

How noble! How truly tolerant! thought Fergus; but how did one offer consolation to a lady who appeared unaware she was in need? Perhaps a gentle hint—? "Lady March, I suspect it may be *worse!*" said he.

Worse than *what?* Nell glanced around in search of her husband, but such was the press of elegant bodies that she had an unobstructed view only of the richly embossed ceiling. "Oh, surely not!" she repeated. "It is all a misunderstanding, mark my words. One must not be too hasty to think oneself trifled with."

"Neither must one blind oneself to the facts," he responded. "Some situations quite surpass human endurance, Lady March!"

What the *devil* was the baron prattling on about? she wondered. It was difficult to concentrate on such a farrago of nonsense when important things were at stake. *How* had Marriot gotten mixed up with stolen jewels? Suddenly she frowned at Fergus. "Good gracious! Is *that* what you're hinting at?"

What Fergus had been hinting at, precisely, was his own keen disapprobation concerning fellows who went about blatantly embracing other fellow's prospective brides, a topic upon which manly modesty forebade him to speak outright. Now that Lady March had grasped his meaning—and mighty calm she was about it!—he fancied he could be a little more direct. "It is. I am sorry you had to learn about it in this way."

In *what* way? She had learned nothing! Eleanor reminded herself that this aggravating young gentleman was a guest in her home, and therefore she was prohibited doing him assault. Not that Nell was ordinarily prone to violence. It was very *hard* to be posed a conundrum, however, when one was already on needles and pins. "I must mingle with my other guests! Pray accompany me, Lord Parrington, so that we may speak further of this."

Never had he known anyone so phlegmatic, decided

Fergus as he followed his hostess down the long room, used long ago as a winter promenade. Past stately buffets and inlaid cabinets and ponderous chests they perambulated, heavy oaken furniture embellished with intricately carved animals and flowers. The baron wondered if Lady March's dégagé attitude was inbred, or born of the discovery that her husband was an inveterate philanderer. How long had Eleanor lived with the scoundrel's peccadilloes? One could hardly ask.

Abruptly, Fergus scowled, having just remembered who Lord March was currently philandering *with*. Where were they? The baron craned his neck. Ah, yes. March had not deserted Mab—who was looking positively adorable in a trained open robe of Salisbury dugget over white sarcenet, and on her curls a charming white lace cap. (Lord March, in mulberry velvet, looked scarcely less fetching, though we must not expect Fergus to appreciate that fact.) Mab appeared to be enjoying herself, Fergus gloomily thought. He had missed her more than he expected. But Lady March was speaking to him. Fergus returned his attention to her ladyship who, in addition to all her jewelry, was wearing an evening robe of black velvet trimmed with gold lace. Were all those jewels conscience gifts from her errant spouse? "Those are prodigious fine jewels you are wearing!" Fergus said.

So he *had* been hinting that he knew something of the jewels! Eleanor clutched the heavy pearl-set golden chain. What did he know, precisely? She must find out! "Let us play no further games with one another!" Nell said sternly. "What is it you're hinting at?"

"I think you know that, Lady March." Fergus watched her sink down amid the embroidered velvet cushions in a square oak chair. "This is a sad business. I extend you my sympathy."

"You—oh!" Fergus must know the jewels had been stolen, else he would not speak in such a manner. "How did you find out?"

A foolish question, surely? Lord Parrington reminded himself that his hostess must be under a grave strain. To tolerate a husband's philandering was one matter; to tolerate it under one's own roof quite another. Scant wonder her ladyship was starting at a sound! How anxiously she looked at him. "You need not fear I shall speak of this," he said kindly. "Not even to my mama! As to how I know of it—Have you forgot? I was there!"

How could she have forgotten what she didn't know? Nell's head began to ache. Had Fergus just admitted he'd been present during the commission of a crime? "Gracious!" Nell gasped.

Fergus realized that her ladyship made a play for time. He could not blame her for hesitating to admit to the perfidious nature of her spouse. "You must see," he murmured, "that I wish to protect Lady Amabel."

"Mab?" Upon this sudden digression, Lady March looked blank. What had Amabel to do with the wretched robberies? "Oh! You do not want her to become involved. But I fear she already *is!* She was determined to be so. And I could not dissuade her, although I confess I did not try very *hard!*"

"You did not?" Lord Parrington in turn sat down abruptly in a Tudor box chair. "Upon my word!"

Why *was* the baron glowering? Nell wished she might give him a sharp pinch. "I do not know why you should find it so difficult to believe! You have a queer notion of the young woman you wished to marry, I think."

Lord Parrington had an even queerer notion of his hostess. "Do you mean to tell me," he hesitantly inquired, "that you don't mind?"

"Mind? Of course I do not mind! Mab has been a great help. I don't know how we would have gone on without her, in fact!" Eleanor made an impatient gesture. "But that is fair and far off! I am a great deal more interested in what you were saying earlier, sir! About my jewels."

What *had* Fergus said about them? He wracked his brain. "They are very fine, but considering the circumstances which led to your possession of them, you would rather not have had them, I am sure."

So he *did* know! But how? Was Lord Parrington on the side of the angels or the devils—Bow Street, in this case? Such distinctions were beyond Nell in this moment. She knew only that Marriot must be told of this without delay.

Furthermore, Henrietta was bearing rapidly down upon them, her wispy hair contained beneath a crepe turban made up in the form of a beehive and finished with a bow, a militant glitter in her eye. "Here is Henrietta! You wish to make her your apologies, Parrington, as I recall!" gasped Nell, and fled.

Apologies for what? Ah yes, sharp speech. Realizing that Henrietta was bound to tell his mama of his presence at the soirée, Fergus was tempted to speak sharper still.

Unaware that she was perilously close to a trimming, Henrietta meantime gazed thoughtfully after the rapidly retreating Eleanor. Nights passed creeping through the drafty corridors of Marcham Towers had in no wise blunted Henrietta's intellect. That Eleanor possessed an abundance of jewels did not surprise Henrietta. But very suspicious she thought it that Nell had suddenly taken to making an exhibition of herself. "I do not see your mama, Parrington!" she archly remarked. "Can it be you are here without her? That is not the act of a considerate son."

On the verge of administering said tongue-lashing, Fergus recalled that, if he antagonized her, Henrietta might well spread stories about Mab. "My mother is indisposed," he therefore replied stiffly. "I will convey your regards."

"You gave her the slip, you mean!" There were few human frailties that Henrietta did not understand. Only in the case of her hosts was she baffled; considering the troubles which beset them, Lord and Lady March remained remarkably calm. Eleanor had not yet fallen victim to a single attack of hysterics despite the presence of her husband's paramour beneath her roof.

If paramour Jane Verney was—but if *not* Marriot's fancy piece, what was she, and why was she here?

Thought of fancy pieces recalled Henrietta to her companion and his apparent attraction to Nell. "Because of your dear mama, I feel it is my duty to drop you a hint, young man! I hope you will not mind if I speak to you like an aunt."

Lord Parrington dared not look upon this presumptious female, lest prudence abandon him. He fixed his attention on another of the Flanders tapestries, a hunting scene which featured an extremely dead hare.

Henrietta took the baron's silence for consent. So pleased was she by the notion of herself as advisor to the peerage that her plump little person puffed up. "To use the word with no bark on it, a gentleman shouldn't allow himself to become overly fond of a lady whose affections are already bestowed elsewhere!"

CHAPTER SEVENTEEN

Due to the vast numbers of people who thronged her long gallery, it was several moments before Lady March reached Amabel. All Nell's guests were anxious to exchange a word with their hostess, most frequently words of an interrogative nature and focused on her spouse. "It is about time you remembered me!" said Mab, deftly extricating Nell from the clutches of a dowager who was waxing enthusiastic about the young prodigy, Master Betty, whom she had recently seen as Hamlet. "I have been trying to catch your attention this age! What *were* you and Fergus talking about at such length?"

Nell frowned at her young friend, who was in tearing spirits. Could she have been mistaken in her interpretation of Lord Parrington's remarks? Nell did not wish to add to the misunderstandings that were already rife. Yet what other explanation could there be for his enigmatic remarks? Fergus apparently not only knew that the jewels she wore were stolen, but that in their theft Marriot had had some part. In truth, thought Nell, Lord Parrington appeared to know more about her husband's recent activities than she did.

Mab still awaited an answer. "I told him you were a great comfort to me. Are you *sure* you wish to marry Parrington, my dear?"

"I am!" Lady Amabel's nature was not so ungenerous as to harbor jealousy. She admired Nell herself, so why should Fergus not? "He'll suit me right down to the ground. Why do you ask?"

It was all Nell could do to keep up with her volatile friend's footsteps, let alone her thoughts. "You said you *wouldn't* marry him; I heard you say so myself! Mab, where are we going?"

Lady Amabel answered these questions in the order they had been presented, all the time inexorably leading Eleanor through the crowd. To insure they were not parted, she kept firm hold of Nell's black velvet dress. "I was out of patience with Fergus when I said I wouldn't marry him; you know what my temper is! Of course I will marry him—once I have decided what to do about his mama, because I *do* refuse to live under the same roof as the old *bat!*"

"How do you mean to accomplish that?" Lady March looked doubtful. "Lord Parrington seems devoted to her."

Mab wrinkled her pretty nose. "What you mean, dear Nell, is that Fergus seems to be neatly under his mama's thumb! I do not deny it! You think Fergus is lacking in spirit, I'll warrant, but that is because you're accustomed to Marriot. I assure you, Fergus is no pudding-heart."

"I did not say he was." Nell doubted a pudding-heart would lend his presence to the commission of a crime. He had not admitted outright that he was involved somehow in the thefts, but what else could his cryptic utterances have meant? "You have not said where we are going, Mab. It is not seemly that I abandon my guests!"

"It will not be for long." Inexorably, Lady Amabel drew Nell out into the hallway. "It will take but a moment to mend your torn lace."

"My lace?" Bewildered, Nell looked down at the gold lace which trimmed her black velvet robe. "But my lace is not torn."

"So it is not." With unabated good cheer, Mab paused, took hold of a swatch of lace, and gave it a good yank. With a very satisfying ripping sound, the lace came loose. Mab grinned. "So much for that! Come along, Nell." Blithely, she continued along the hallway.

Lady March had scant choice but to follow, clutching her torn lace, wondering what bee Mab had taken under her pretty lace cap. Not until they approached the sewing room did she guess. "Oh! You are very clever, Mab."

In a very vulgar manner, Lady Amabel winked. "Ain't I just?" she agreed, and flung open the sewing room door.

Framed in the opened portal, Jane sat near the fireplace on a little stool. Glimpsing the ladies, she got up and dropped an awkward curtsey. Then she caught a closer glimpse of Lady March. Her lower jaw dropped open, her eyes protruded, her pale skin turned as colorless as parchment.

It was the briefest of lapses, consternation stifled almost as quickly as it had appeared, yet it left neither Mab nor Nell in any further doubt. "Lady March has torn her lace," Mab said smoothly before Nell could speak.

"So I see, miss. I'll just fix it, shall I?" Already Jane had taken needle and thread in hand, had bent to her task. Eleanor forced herself to stand motionless while Jane repaired the lace, her impulse to give vent to temper quelled by the monstrous faces Mab made behind Jane's back. "There! All's bowman, ma'am!" said Jane as she stepped back.

Bowman, was it? Whatever that meant! This from the odious wench her husband had allegedly led astray? As if Marriot *would!* "Thank you, Jane!" responded Nell in unsteady tones. "It was stupidly done of me!" Need for further conversation was spared her by Mab, who whisked her back out into the hallway and closed the door.

"Put her in a tweak, did we not?" Looking very triumphant, Lady Amabel executed a lively little dance step. "I thought her eyes were going to pop right out of her head! She *did* come here looking for the jewels, just like we suspected. We must tell Marriot!"

"So we must," agreed Eleanor, whose aspect was a great deal less jubilant than Mab's. Was it possible that Jane and Lord Parrington were in league? Some connection must exist between them, since both knew about the jewels. Yet one could not envision the

141

starched-up baron under any circumstances rubbing shoulders with the very common Jane.

Lord March was at length discovered in the long gallery, enthroned in a Tudor box chair of ample proportions embellished with mythological figures entwined with birds and beasts and flowers. By way of various energetic motions, Lady Amabel caught his attention, as well as that of various other guests. Politely, Marriot disengaged himself from chair and guests alike and came forward. "What is it, brat?"

Mab grinned, "Don't put on that stern face with me, Marriot! I'll warrant you are glad of the rescue. Moreover, we have the *most* exciting news!"

Lord March glanced from Lady Amabel's animated countenance to his wife's beloved features, the perfection of which was marred by a slight frown. "She rose to the bait!" he said slowly. "You are to be felicitated with upon the cleverness of your ploy, brat—but *now* what?"

Mab linked her arms with those of Lord and Lady March. "Now you must take Nell and me down to supper, Marriot!"

Intrigued as Lord March was by Lady Amabel's disclosures, he did not overlook his duties as host. It was some time later—his lordship's guests being almost unanimously determined to discuss such topics as tinkers and press gangs and foreign agents—before he had further opportunity to speak privately with Mab and his wife. During that interval, Lady March and Amabel had an interesting encounter of their own with a dowager dressed in purple satin, rouge on her cheeks and feathers in her hair.

"Hah!" said the dowager, staring at Eleanor's jewell-laden chest. "Aren't *we* decked out in full rig! Why did I have it in my head that you didn't care for jewels, Eleanor? Marriot has done right by you, I must say!" The better to survey her hostess's bosom, she elevated her quizzing glass. "Demned if those pearls don't look like the ones I had stolen—good Gad, gal, don't go so pasty on us! I didn't mean *you'd* took the things!"

142

"Of course you did not, Lady Agatha!" Solicitously, Mab took Nell's arm and covertly gave her a sharp pinch. "Nell has been made very nervous by all these thefts, thinking she may be *next!* That is why she has worn so many of her jewels all at once—but tell us how the robbery came about!" The dowager was not reluctant. Zestfully, she related her set-to with villains, which had taken place on a dark street in a remote section of the city, on a dark and moonless night.

"The links boy was next to useless!" Lady Agatha concluded in disgust. "Took to his heels when the scroundrels came forth with their pistols at the ready, and with him took the light. My people put up a stout enough defense, but they were outnumbered."

"Ruffians?" Lest Nell's courage desert her, Mab pinched her again. "There were several of them, then? Masked, I'll warrant? I thought they must have been! You see, Nell, that your jewels are safe enough, so long as you refrain from going out into dark streets. But there is Marriot, beckoning to us! Excuse us, Lady Agatha, pray." The dowager regally inclined her head. Mab led Lady March away. "Nell," she hissed, "if you swoon I shall *never* speak to you again!"

"Oh, do leave off pinching at me, Mab!" snapped Eleanor, jerking her arm away. Due to the dowager's confidences, Nell was much closer to hysteria than Amabel had guessed.

This conversation took place in the dining room of Marcham Towers, just off the great hall, where delicate and choice refreshments of every kind had been set out buffet style. The guests had not lost interest in Marriot, precisely, but were so overwhelmed by the feast set out on the seven-foot-long drawtop table that they temporarily ceased to badger their host.

Said Lady Amabel as she and Nell joined Marriot at one of the small tables set up around the room, "We have learned a prodigious lot! Lady Agatha recognized Nell's pearls—Do not look so horrified! You are as bad as Nell, Marriot! Since no one would ever credit Nell with filching anything, we are perfectly safe."

143

"Safe, are we?" Lord March arranged himself in a panel-back chair. "You are of an over-optimistic nature, brat!"

Lady Amabel made a moue: "And *you* are a spoil-sport, Marriot! Do you not realize what this means? Jane does not work alone!" She paused so that her companions might share in her enthusiasm. They did not. Undeterred, Mab continued, "Now that we are certain Jane came here in search of the jewels, we must plan what to do next. I *had* thought of simply turning her over to the authorities, but it would be her word against ours; and while I am reasonably certain no one would believe her, I think we should have proof. And we should make a push to round up her confederates. Beside," and Mab wrinkled her pretty nose, "'twould be a very lame ending for our adventures!"

Lady March gazed without enthusiasm upon her tray supper of chicken and champagne. Mab would be a great deal less enthusiastic did she realize Jane had not been the only person to react suspiciously to the gems. "I knew I should never have let Henrietta talk me into having that female in the house!" she moaned.

"Darling Nell!" Lord March grasped her hand. "This business will soon be over—and then I will make up to you for every *instant* of discomfort you have endured on my behalf!"

"Oh, Marriot!" Eleanor placed her other hand atop his. "As if you *needed* to! Why—"

"Fiddlestick!" Having polished off her own plate, Lady Amabel gave the plates of her companions a covetous glance. "Next you will tell Marriot you are *glad* to be made unhappy on his account, which is a great piece of nonsense, Nell! No one can be glad to be made unhappy unless they are very much of an oddity! As for Jane, Henrietta served us a very good turn by taking up the cudgels on her behalf. I know you cannot like her, Nell—and scant wonder! I do not like her myself!—but Jane is the only way we can learn the truth about the jewels."

Jane was not quite the *only* way, thought Nell; of all

144

the people possibly looking for Marriot in connection with the jewels, she had never thought Lord Parrington might be one. Nell glanced around the dining room and glimpsed Fergus seated at a distant table with Henrietta. What were they discussing? Henrietta looked very animated, and the baron grim. What would Fergus do now he had confirmed Marriot's possession of the stolen gems?

"What a coil!" Nell said aloud, and shoved aside her untouched plate. "Next I suppose Henrietta will take to confiding to her cronies that she knew all along Marriot was not in Cornwall—and how we are to wrap *that* in clean linen I do not know!"

Lord March expressed an ignoble wish to wrap his cousin in linen—to wit, her own shroud. "We must not borrow trouble, puss! Henrietta will dare not be that malicious so long as she remains beneath our roof."

Not surprisingly, Eleanor's black mood was not lightened by this reminder that Henrietta's sojourn was like to prove of long duration. She sighed.

"Sweet Nell!" murmured Marriot, who had been puzzling over his elusive memory of a red silk bonnet. "I *shall* make it up to you, I vow!"

Lady Amabel, the only member of this small group to evidence an appetite, had occupied herself during this exchange by nodding at the passing guests and cleaning off all three plates. Temporarily replete, she touched a fringed napkin to her lips. "I do wish the two of you would cease to make sheep's eyes at one another!" she remarked.

Thus abjured, Lord and Lady March looked guiltily elsewhere. Since both were temporarily out of charity with Lady Amabel, conversation flagged.

Though remarks between Lord and Lady March and Lady Amabel had ground down to a halt, talk elsewhere flowed as lavishly as his lordship's wine, and the guests circulated freely around the dining room. This chamber, with its low exposed rafters and mullioned windows and linenfold paneling, was made cozy by a stone fireplace with pilasters and semi-raised work. Most

145

outstanding among its many antique furnishings was a huge court cupboard which served as a sideboard for displaying a vast array of treasures, including silver plate and pewter, vases of gold and crystal and myrrh wood from Arabia, all set out on Turkey cloth. Not all such treasures were confined to the court cupboard. The guests ate from exquisite dishes, drank from goblets fashioned of Venetian glass.

Having emptied her own goblet, Mab set it aside. "Now that Jane knows the jewels are in the house, she will try even harder to get them back."

"Wonderful," said Nell, with unabated gloom. "I will not dare close my eyes at night, for fear the creature may go poking about beneath my bed. Why do we not just *give* her the wretched things, and tell her to leave?"

Lord March twirled his own goblet, which had been filled with nothing less innocuous than water, his lordship being in great need of a clear head. "That would not solve the puzzle of how I came by the jewels in the first place, Nell—a puzzle about which I admit myself very curious! If there is a hangman in my future, I would prefer to be prepared. My darling, do not look so horrified! I spoke in jest."

Reminded of their guests, Lady March lowered her stricken gaze from her husband's rueful features to her own hands clenched in her lap. "I beg you will never say such a thing again, even in fun, Marriot! You *hanged?*" She shuddered. "I cannot bear the thought."

"It will not come to that!" soothed his lordship. "I promise you, Nell."

Her ladyship was not so easily consoled. "That's all well and good," she muttered, "but you have also told me that if you *are* guilty, you will take your punishment!"

This somewhat inane discussion could continue indefinitely, decided Lady Amabel. "Have you decided Marriot *is* guilty, Nell? No? Then pray cease to enact us a Cheltenham tragedy! And don't *you* scold me for speaking so, Marriot! We were deciding what should be done about Jane, you will recall. No, Nell, we must not push her out a window! You are funning me, I think."

In point of fact, Lady March had not been funning, but her brief homicidal mania did not last. "Why don't we just let her 'find' the wretched things? And if Jane came here expecting that we had the jewels, why was she so astonished to see me wearing them?"

"Jane knows they are stolen." Mab pushed back her chair. "If we had not already guessed she came here in search of the jewels, there would be our proof. You still do not understand, do you Nell? A person caught in possession of stolen jewels could go to gaol. As for letting Jane 'find' the jewels—that would leave our questions unanswered. We would be no nearer knowing how Marriot came by the things."

"Gaol!" Lady March's expression was wry. "Marriot is right; you *are* a brat! Do not bother telling me I must be prepared to make sacrifices on Marriot's behalf, Mab; naturally I am! But I do *not* know that I am prepared to go to gaol in his place."

"Are you not, my darling?" inquired Lord March in disappointed tones. "You wound me! I made sure that, if push came to shove, you would go to Newgate in my place."

Had she failed her husband? Stricken, Nell glanced quickly up into his face. "Wretch!" she retorted, reassured by the twinkle in his eye. "This is a dreadful fix, Marriot! I don't know how you can joke."

"I fear I am a frivolous fellow." A certain grim note in his lordship's voice gave this blithe statement the lie. "Mab was telling us how we must deal with Jane. Continue, brat!"

"One almost has to admire the creature." Mab toyed with her empty goblet. "Forcing her way into the house as she did—she is as bold as brass! She's also no pea-goose. We'll need to keep our wits about us—or Marriot will."

"I will?" Lord March responded warily to this assertion. "Why is that?"

Mab smiled and rose, preparatory to returning to the heavily laden drawtop table for some hothouse fruit and cheese. "Because, Marriot, your memory is about to return!"

CHAPTER EIGHTEEN

Cautiously, Jane stepped into the solar and glanced around. A cursory inspection assured her that no one hovered by the oriel window or lurked by the fireplace. Save for Lord March, engaged in contemplation of the caterpillar embroidered on the chair on which he sat, she was quite alone.

He did not rise to greet her, Jane noted, as she took up a position a prudent distance from his lordship— not that she had expected to be treated like one of the nobs. In all her life, no one had risen when Jane entered a room, and very queer she would have thought it if they had. Very queer, in fact, Jane thought many of the goings-on in Marcham Towers. To say nothing of the house itself, she silently added, eyeing the carved Diana bathing on the fireplace.

Lord March was watching her, Jane discovered when she looked away. The quality of his attention put her on guard. She dropped a curtsey. "You wished to see me, sir?"

"You have left me little choice but to see you." Marriot's tone was dry. "I think that you have been telling taradiddles, Jane."

Taradiddles, was it? Jane was indeed no peagoose, and thus suspected that Lord March's errant memory had in some measure returned. But in *what* measure? "Ah! That's as may be, sir. Mayhap if you was to open your budget, I'd know what we was talking about!"

Lord March appeared most interested in his gleaming boots, one of which he had propped comfortably upon an opposite knee. "I would think that was clear enough. You see, I have regained my memory, Jane!" He directed a reproving glance at her. "Oddly, I do *not* remember leading you astray."

Was his lordship angry? Jane pleated the drab dark stuff of her skirt. "It seemed," she cautiously admitted, "like a good notion at the time! I had to say *some*thing, afore that platter-faced female turned me out—beggin' your pardon, sir!"

"No need." Lord March made an expansive gesture. "Henrietta *is* platter-faced. And abominably inquisitive! I have often been tempted to tell her taradiddles myself. There was no harm done. In truth, I should thank you for it, because had you *not* told Henrietta that you and I were close acquaintances, I would not have regained my memory. Oh, I might eventually have regained it, but not in this same manner, because my wife would have had no reason to hit me over the head!"

"Hit you?" A suspicious nature did not prevent Jane appreciating a good yarn. "Lawks! When I told that clanker, I didn't know you was leg-shackled to a tempersome female, sir! Very sorry I am if I've put your missus in a tweak, because she seems a very fine lady—not but what I never thought ladies went about hitting people on the head. Though I daresay in her place I'd have acted similar—no offense intended!"

Marriot suspected strongly that Jane *had* done the same, in at least one instance, and was very curious about her motivation. "Let us lay our cards on the table!" he invited. "Knowing I had lost my memory, you secured access to my house."

"Aye." For a gentleman determined to have things out in the open, Lord March was being very circumspect. Jane decided it would behoove her to be equally discreet. "I *don't* have a mag with which to bless myself—that much of what I said was true. Knowing you to be an open-fisted bloke, I banked you'd help me raise the wind."

So now he was become philanthropist to the city's unfortunate females? Marriot stretched his long legs before him. "Whatever you banked on, Jane, I think it was not that. You are not all to pieces—which reminds me, I have not properly thanked you for, er, preventing me from prematurely turning up my toes!"

"No need!" Jane's bland expression did not reveal her growing conviction that his lordship's erratic memory had not entirely returned. "Proper grateful you was at the time. And very poorly you repaid me for it, moreover! But if you was to snack the bit, I'd shove my trunk and forget all about this little misunderstanding. *I* ain't one to hold a grudge!"

Snack the bit? Hop the twig? Marriot's unexplained knowledge of such esoteric phrases came to his rescue: Jane had just offered, did he but share the money with her, to go away. *What* money? The proceeds of robbery, Marriot feared. Though every instinct rebelled at the suggestion they had been lovers, he apparently knew Jane a great deal better than he should. "And what if I do not care to, er, 'snack the bit'?" he inquired.

This suggestion found no favor with Jane. "Cor!" she gasped. "Damned if you *ain't* an out-and-out rogue. You should be chary of these queer turns you take, or you'll find yourself being taken for a criminal offense. Not that *I'll* ride grub, but I can't promise someone else won't nab the rust." Just how much *had* his lordship remembered? "There was the devil of a rowdy-do when it was discovered the sparklers had been pinched."

That much Marriot could easily visualize. Was Jane saying that *he* had filched the jewels? "I suppose a great many people are angry with me," he said plaintively. "I did not think of that."

His lordship had not thought of several things, mused Jane as she eyed a studded, quilted stool; among them that she might welcome an opportunity to rest her bones. Jane's sojourn in Marcham Towers had been neither idle nor luxurious, and she was not accustomed to the exhausting nature of honest toil. Nor, truth be told, did she care for it. Jane's recent experience with the straight and narrow led her to seriously question why anyone would choose that path. "You know what you may do to make amends!" she said. "Give the sparklers back."

151

So that the gems might immediately disappear into London's teeming underworld? Marriot thought not. Though he knew little of such matters, he realized that did he simply hand over the gems to Jane neither he nor the rightful owners would see the jewels again. They would resurface, eventually, but in greatly altered form. Or *did* he know little of such matters? It was proving deuced difficult to find out. Perhaps a different approach might serve him better. Marriot rose from his chair and approached a decanter which he had had the foresight to previously set out.

Jane was not adverse to a dram taken so early in the day, indeed quaffed it at a gulp. She was no more appealing at close quarters than at a distance, Marriot decided. Lest she prove to be responsible for the recent frequent assaults upon his head, he stepped warily back and leaned against one of several wall panels decorated with landscapes. "We are not proceeding very quickly," he observed after sampling his own glass.

So they were not; Jane had already realized that despite his assertions to the contrary, his lordship's memory wasn't in prime twig. Not that she cared a button about his lordship's memory. What Jane wanted was to speedily remove the jewels—and herself!—from this depressingly grand house. To this end, she silently held out her glass.

Marriot refilled it, as well as his own. "We both know that I have *not* been in Cornwall, following a quarrel with my wife."

"Aye, sir." Appreciatively, Jane sloshed the wine around in her mouth before swallowing audibly. "That we do!"

Here was heavy going! Marriot took another sip. "And both of us know what I was actually up to!"

Unquestionably, both of them did not, thought Jane. "Cor!" she said, and licked her lips. "If this don't bring back memories! Many is the time we've shared a rumstick of bob slim—not that I mean to impose, you understand!"

Lord March understood that the drink thus referred

to was a certain quantity of punch. He eyed his alleged drinking partner, and then his own glass. Looking very cheerful, Jane boldy hefted the decanter. "Or," she added, for good measure, "a flag's worth of lightening— you remember, sir, fourpence of gin! But I'll be as close as oysters! No one will learn from *me* that Lord March did what he should not!"

"No one that has not already," his lordship amended wryly. "You could hardly do worse by me than you have already done—but never mind that! I am still waiting for you to lay your cards on the table, Jane."

Cards it was his lordship wanted? Jane prepared to withdraw an ace from up her sleeve. "I *am* sorry, sir," she said sadly, "but you know you'll have to give the sparklers back! Very angry the lads were when they discovered you'd sloped off—very unsporting they thought it, seeing as it was all your idea!"

"*My* idea!" Lord March sought refuge from this appalling suggestion in his own wineglass.

"*Your* idea!" Jane was quick to recognize her advantage. "I ain't one not to give credit where it's due. 'Twas your idea entirely as you must remember, and you were set on it even when I told you how you could be hobbled—taken up, that is, and committed for trial!"

"Trial," echoed his lordship faintly, still peering into his glass. Solicitously, Jane filled it. "You jest."

"As if I would!" Jane looked reproachful. "About a thing like *that!* Oh, I knew how it was with you, from the beginning, that you was one for queer turns—but that ain't something as can be easily explained to the lads! A proper take-in, they think it—and I can tell you they don't take kindly to having been gulled! 'Twas all I could do to prevent them taking matters into their own hands."

What might be done to him by ruffians who thought him a traitor Lord March could not imagine, but he did not imagine the experience would be nice. No coward, and no weakling, Marriot was not overly concerned by the suggestion that physical violence might be offered him. His wife's sensibilities, however, were more acute.

Marriot frowned at the red-painted wainscoting touched out in gold and blue.

His lordship, thought Jane, was a little the worse for drink—not that he should be condemned for it, having consumed a fair quantity of wine on an empty stomach and very early in the day. As had, in fact, Jane; but Jane had a very hard head. "The lads *said* they'd like to use your guts for fiddlestrings!" she added. "I don't know how long I can hold them off. Give the sparklers back, do! I'll hand them over to the lads and no further harm done. It ain't like you're under the hatches yourself!"

Lord March thought he was like to be worse than under the hatches. "You are telling me, that while in temporary loss of my memory I embarked upon a life of crime."

Just as she had thought! His lordship *had* put forth a great amount of humbug in an effort to catch her out. Jane was not so easily done for. "Why should I be after telling you what you already know?" she asked. "Give over, guv'nor! Wasn't I right at your shoulder when you planned the things out?"

Slightly inebriated as Marriot might be, he was not sufficiently cast away to believe that he had ever, for any purpose, even temporarily allied himself with this whey-faced female. "The devil you were!" he snapped.

"Then I wasn't, sir! Whatever you say!" Jane clasped her hands, and her empty glass, to her bosom. "Don't hit me, I beg you! I'll stand buff and won't squeal, I swear it—just don't take a distempered freak!"

"Take a *what?*" Carefully, Lord March set down his glass. "What in the blazes are you talking about?"

"Oh sir, have you forgot poor Dickon? Not that I should wonder at it, because if anyone was ever after forgetting anything, it'd be that he left someone floating facedown in the Thames! Not that I'm saying you *shouldn't* have; it ain't my place." Jane presented an excellent enactment of terror. Had not a life of crime held out more appeal—and potential profit!—she might have done very well upon the stage.

"Good God!" Lord March's voice was faint. "Are you saying I *killed* a man?"

"Not if you don't want me to!" Jane responded promptly. "Do be a good fellow and hand over the sparklers, sir, so that I can give them back to the lads. Then you'll hear no more of us, I swear it—no, or of poor Dickon either! Mayhap you don't know what happens to thieves, but I do, and you wouldn't like it above half!"

Nor did Lord March especially like his present fix. All the same, he was not disposed to meekly hand over the jewels. "Yes, well, I can't!" he responded, with a flash of the imaginative reasoning that habitually inspired him in the wake of strong drink. "They aren't in the house!"

"*Aren't?*" Jane's eyes narrowed. "That won't fadge. I saw her ladyship wearing some of them last night."

"*Some* of them, Jane!" Having finally gained control of the situation, Lord March propped an elbow against his gaily painted wainscoting and prepared to enjoy himself. "Surely you don't think me so very great a flat as to have them in my house."

Jane had thought precisely that. No wonder her diligent searching had been to no avail! "Where then?" she inquired.

Lord March elevated a cautionary forefinger. "In a very secret place!" he replied. "So secret that I cannot tell even *you* about it, Jane! I will give you back the jewels, but first I must retrieve them. You must tell me where the transfer will take place."

Did his lordship think her a pigeon for the plucking? Little did he know the shoe was on the other foot. "I'll think on it!" Jane promised, and abruptly departed the solar.

Lord March was also thinking, so very hard that for several moments after Jane's departure he stared broodingly upon the wainscoting. Then he became aware that the wainscoting was quivering in a highly suspect manner. Hastily, he removed his elbow and stepped back.

First to step through the secret opening was Lady

155

Amabel, liberally festooned with cobwebs and clutching the ancient Toledo walking sword. Behind her came Lady March, who no sooner emerged than she flung herself into her husband's arms. "We heard all!" she cried. "Oh, Marriot!"

"Nell, do hush!" Mab's impatience resulted from the interval she had just endured, with Nell whispering laments in her unreceptive ear. "Do you not realize that the fox is on the run? Finally we are making progress!"

Lady March had scant interest in either foxes or progress, clutched her husband so tightly that he found it difficult to draw breath. "Are we, indeed! Didn't you hear what that odious female said about what happens to thieves?"

"I heard a great deal more than *you* did!" Mab retorted, brandishing her sword. "You spent most of the time muttering in my ear—and very difficult that makes it to concentrate, I must say! Oh Nell, we must not quarrel! Now is the time to put our heads together, so that we will be ready for Jane's next move. She will suggest a meeting place, depend on it! We must decide what we will do then. Go through with it, I think, and at least pretend to turn over the jewels, and then—"

"And then allow her to dispose of Marriot!" So indignant was Nell made by this suggestion that she released her husband, who inhaled a deep breath. "One might think it was *you* who had shot the cat, Mab!"

This suggestion found favor with its recipient, who helped herself to wine. "Come down off your high ropes, Nell! Our Jane is too shrewd to dispose of Marriot until after she has made certain he returned all the gems, which he will not. So long as Marriot alone knows the whereabouts of the jewels, he is safe. Now we need only determine the story *we* mean to tell, because there is bound to be a certain amount of notoriety involved with the thieves being brought to justice."

Should she speak? Nell thought she must. "More notoriety than you might think, Mab." Solicitously,

Nell clasped her friend's hands, regardless of walking sword and wineglass. "I wish I did not have to tell you, but I am very much afraid that Parrington is involved in this business."

CHAPTER NINETEEN

"Business? Involved in what business? What the *deuce* are you talking about, Mab?" Lord Parrington looked uneasily about him. "And why the deuce are we *here,* and at this hour of night?"

"Pray lower your voice," Lady Amabel replied. "I shall explain everything. As for why we're here, it is because Henrietta decided she must attend the theater with us, which has made Marriot late! Of all nights for her to grow suspicious! But Nell did not wish Marriot to come alone, so it has all worked out for the best."

This latter optimistic assertion Fergus took leave to doubt. As for Henrietta's suspicions, he could not blame her; anyone must be made very curious by the sight of four well-dressed people strolling about an unfashionable part of the city, one of them clutching an antique walking sword, in the midst of a dense fog. Fergus was only surprised that Henrietta had elected to remain in the carriage and await their return. Fergus's own instincts for duplicity had been alerted by the extremely lame explanation of their untimely perambulations, that Lord March had a personal errand to execute. Given his lordship's penchant for disappearing, it was no wonder Lady March did not care to have him undertake his errand without escort.

Other instincts, however, had precedence, and Mab looked very lovely, a velvet evening cloak concealing her gown of sprigged muslin, and a handkerchief cap of muslin and lace ornamented with a wreath of roses upon her dark hair. "I wish you *would* explain," he said, cautiously eyeing her walking sword. "What the devil are you doing with that thing?"

"Protecting you, dear Fergus!" Mab grinned and flourished the sword. "Don't pucker up; I *wasn't* calling you a dull stick! No, and I didn't mean it even when I *did* call you one, but you had made me angry by hinting you *didn't* wish to marry me. But we will talk about *that* another time. Right now, I must ask you— Fergus, is it true that you know about the jewels?"

"The *what?*" This odd question recalled the baron's straying attention from their surroundings and the thick fog. No lack of appreciation of his companion had occassioned Fergus's lapse, but the neighborhood through which they walked, an area of mean alleys and narrow courts—precisely the sort of neighborhood in which one might be set upon by footpads.

"The jewels!" Mab repeated, impatiently. "Do pay attention, Fergus! Did you or did you not tell Nell that you not only knew the wretched things were stolen, but that you were present at the time?"

"Stolen?" Fergus wondered if his hearing might have been affected by the dense mist. "Did you say *stolen*, Mab?"

"I did." The baron looked positively toasty, thought Mab, in his ankle-length many-caped Garrick overcoat. With the intention of hinting he should share that warmth she moved closer. Due to the resultant proximity of the Toledo walking sword, Lord Parrington backed away.

"Oh!" Mab's pretty face was sad. "You *don't* want to marry me! Or can it be you think I meant it when I said I didn't wish to marry *you?*"

Lord Parrington recalled Lady March's comments on the topic of philandering spouses. "We'll talk about *that* another time also!" he remarked. "Just now I am much more interested in these jewels."

Fergus was more interested in jewels than in her? Briefly, Mab's heart sank. However, she was of a resilient nature, and smack in the middle of an adventure, and tomorrow was time enough to decide whether or not she had a broken heart. "Are you trying to tell me that you *don't* know about them? Then why did you tell Nell you *did?*" she asked.

"I *didn't* tell her so!" Lord Parrington wondered if

the lady whose forebearance he had so admired was in fact quite mad. "I said only that I understood why March had given her them, poor soul!"

"But if you understood that Nell was wearing the jewels to try and flush out the thieves," argued Mab, "you must have known the jewels were stolen in the first place!" She observed his consternation. "I do not know *what* to make of this, Fergus!"

Neither did the baron. "Was that why you sent word that I should make up a member of this party? Because you thought I knew something about stolen gems?"

Mab wrinkled her pretty nose. "What a muddle!" she sighed. "I thought that if you *were* involved in this business somehow, I wanted you where I could keep an eye on you—and I will tell you frankly, Fergus, that I am not certain you are not!"

Lord Parrington, in that moment, was not certain himself, a circumstance that led him to wonder if his own memory had lapsed. For assurance that it had not, he applied to Lady March. Rather, he tried to do so. Several paces ahead of Fergus and Lady Amabel, Eleanor was currently engaged in a heated discussion with her spouse. "I do not believe it!" she was heard to cry. "I *cannot* believe it! You could not have done away with someone, Marriot!"

"Done *away* with?" echoed Lord Parrington, aghast.

There was nothing for it, then, but that explanations be put forth. The party paused beneath a feeble street-lamp. "Marriot did *not* leave someone floating facedown in the Thames!" insisted Nell, adopting a belligerent stance. "And if he did, I'm sure he had an excellent reason for it. Perhaps you may acquaint us with that reason, Parrington, since you know so much about this business—perhaps you were present then as well!"

This was the female whose great good sense he had admired? "As well as *when?*" Fergus cautiously inquired.

"As well as—oof!" Recalled by Mab's sharp elbow to her surroundings, Nell glanced nervously over her shoulder. "You know what I mean! You said yourself that you were there!"

Lord Parrington rubbed his brow. "I said I was *where?* We seem to be laboring under a certain confusion of ideas. The only jewels I know anything about are yours, Lady March." He awarded Marriot an uncomplimentary glance. "Given you as conscience gifts."

"Conscience—oho!" Mab clapped her gloved hands. "I believe I begin to understand!"

"Then pray share your enlightenment with the rest of us," begged Lord March, who did not like to be regarded as if he were the fiend incarnate. "For your information, Parrington, I do not *need* to give my wife conscience gifts, not because I lack a conscience, but because I have done nothing wrong!" Recalling Jane's assertions to the contrary, he frowned. "I think!"

"Oh, Marriot!" gasped Eleanor, clutching his arm. "I *know* you have not!" This single-minded devotion earned her a fond smile. "Darling Nell!" murmured his lordship.

"'Darling'?" echoed Lord Parrington, staring puzzled upon this touching tableau. Lady March had not the least look of a person set on keeping up appearances, nor Lord March of a philanderer. Then he glanced at Mab. "I don't understand any of this!" Fergus confessed. "I thought, from various things that Lady March said, that you and Lord March—Well!"

"Marriot and *me?*" Mab giggled at the notion. "You are thinking that you saw Marriot hug me, but I have known him all my life! Marriot has frequently hugged me—yes, and spanked me on occasion, as I recall! Do not look so horrified; I am certain I deserved it. But you must not go on thinking I have been compromised, by either Marriot or yourself." This was hardly a setting conducive to getting up a flirtation, but she did have Fergus's undivided attention. Mab fluttered her long eyelashes. "You are not *obliged* to marry me, Fergus. However, if you still *wish* to ..." The baron ignored this unsubtle hint, and Mab's voice trailed off. She then discovered that they had attracted a small audience.

This neighborhood being neither haunt nor habitat of the Upper Ten Thousand, that audience was neither of the chosen nor the best. In point of fact, it was raucous and a little offensive. With a pointed flourish of her walking sword, Mab suggested they continue on their way.

"I think I understand how our misunderstanding came about!" said Nell over her shoulder to Fergus. "We must have been talking at cross purposes. When I was referring to the jewels, you thought I spoke of something else." She frowned. "That has me in a puzzle! What could you think I was talking about?"

"Er!" responded the baron, too much of a gentleman—and also too embarrassed—to make reference to a supposedly errant spouse. "Shouldn't we be getting back to the carriage? Your cousin will think we have got lost."

"Not until Marriot has kept his rendezvous!" explained Mab, while Lord March voiced a pious wish that his cousin might get lost. "He is pretending to give back the jewels, you see! He isn't, really; but we have decided this is the only way to discover how he came by them in the first place."

"In the first place," echoed Fergus, his bewilderment abated not one whit. As if to mitigate that confusion, Lord March genially gestured toward the shabby valise which was largely obscured by his handsome fur-lined redingote. "The jewels *are* stolen, then?"

"Oh, yes!" said Mab, paying close attention to her skirts. The narrow street which they traversed was neither sweet-smelling nor in good repair. "It only remains to determine by *whom!*"

"It wasn't Marriot!" inserted Lady March in a voice that was very grim. *"I* know Marriot never stole anything in all his life, no matter what anyone else may say!"

Fergus had no desire to argue with Lady March. "But if March didn't steal the things—and I'm not saying he did!—then who was responsible for the thefts?"

he whispered to Mab. His query earned him an approving glance.

"*That,*" said Mab, "is what we are about to find out! Marriot, are we not almost there? Should we not wait while you proceed without us, lest Jane become alarmed? Do not go into the fidgets, Nell; 'twill all be over soon enough. Anyway, you know Marriot is armed!"

"So I am." Comfortingly, Lord March patted his wife. "And you are correct, as usual, Mab. Wait you here, where you will not be noticed, while I go to keep my, er, tête-à-tête."

"I only hope it is a tête-à-tête," muttered Nell, but made no effort to detain him. Marriot bent to kiss her cheek, then stepped out into the fog. Briefly, silence descended upon the three who remained behind.

The night itself was far from silent despite the muffling effect of the dense mist. This narrow street and those which intersected it were well-traveled by creatures of the night. That the fog prevented her taking a closer look at the passersby, Mab could not regret. Some things a maiden was better off not seeing, even a maiden not possessed of overly delicate sensibilities. The carryings-on of that slattern on the corner opposite, for example, who was clutching a male companion with one hand and with the other a bottle of gin.

Those goings-on, deplore them as Mab might, set up a train of thought. Mab took hold of the lowest of Lord Parrington's many capes and tugged. "Fergus, are you *sorry* you kissed me?" she asked.

The baron glanced with some astonishment down into Mab's wistful face. "Sorry? Of course not!"

He had answered without the slightest hesitation, Mab was pleased to note. "Then *that's* all right!" she sighed.

Lady March, meantime, peered into the fog, following her husband's stalwart figure to the limits of her vision, and causing herself considerable eyestrain. He strolled toward a well-lighted building, which stood out pale and ghostly in the mist. By the windows of that building many figures passed and paused—even posed, thought Nell. Squinting, she tried to make the figures out. "Good God!" she said aloud, stricken by the belated realization that she observed a bawdy house.

Mab, in lieu of a similar realization, interpreted Lady March's ejaculation in light of past experience. "Nell, pray do not be a peagoose! Marriot has the situation well in hand, I promise you! Do continue, Fergus! Was there something you wished to say?"

Had he meant to say something? Fergus could not remember. He folded his arms across his chest, doubting he would ever again be warm. There was an unexceptionable topic of conversation! "How long must we wait here?" he plaintively inquired.

"Only until Marriot returns to us." Mab wondered if Lord Parrington might be persuaded to hug her as opposed to himself.

Still Nell stared intently into the thick mist. Occasionally the fog thinned sufficiently for her to glimpse Marriot. He had paused on the streetcorner as instructed, was waiting for contact to be made—but what was this? Two men crept up behind him. Nell's voice came out a thin croak. "Marriot!"

Lady Amabel awarded her friend a stern look. "I *told* you not to—" She followed Nell's pointing finger, saw Marriot knocked unconscious and dragged across the street. "Eek!"

"'Eek!' Is that all you can say? 'Eek'?" Nell grabbed up her skirts, prepared to follow her senseless spouse to the ends of the earth. "Why do you hold me back, Mab? We must do something straightaway!"

"So we must." Thoughtfully, Mab eyed Fergus. "I think the *first* thing we must do is notify Bow Street. The time for secrecy is past."

"*You* notify Bow Street!" Futilely, Nell sought to free herself from Mab's restraining hands. "Let me go *instantly!* You would not like it if Parrington was incarcerated in a bawdy house, I daresay!"

"A bawdy house? Is *that* what one looks like?" Fascinated, Mab stared. "Do calm yourself, Nell! Nothing so very dreadful is apt to happen to Marriot with so

164

many people around. Hurry, Fergus, I beg you! Nell and I will wait right here until you come back." She thrust the walking sword at him. "Here! Take this, just in case!"

Lord Parrington did not relish the notion of making his solitary way through a London fog, and suspected he would be greeted with derision at Bow Street Public Office. A nobleman kidnapped into a brothel? It did make an unlikely tale. But Mab was looking at him with a mixture of supplication and impatience. If he refused she would doubtless make further adverse comments upon his character. Too, Lord March *was* likely in danger—and was that a carriage he heard approaching, Henrietta's querulous tones calling out? Abruptly, he plunged into the fog.

Lord Parrington's departure was not a moment premature. *"There* you are!" cried Henrietta, her head stuck out the carriage window, the ostrich plumes of her headdress sadly bedraggled by the damp. "I thought you had got lost! Why did Parrington leave in that queer abrupt manner? And where is Marriot?" No answer to these questions was forthcoming. Nell moaned.

Eleanor having proven uncommunicative, Henrietta turned her fire on Lady Amabel, who was acting no less odd. Stunned, Henrietta watched Mab pull off her rose-wreathed lace and muslin cap, fling back her velvet cloak, take hold of the buffont of lace that adorned the bosom of her sprigged evening dress. "What *are* you doing, child?" she gasped.

Ruthlessly, Mab ripped away her lace, thus altering her bodice to expose a lush expanse of creamy skin. Smugly, she gazed upon her astonished audience. Mysteriously she whispered, "I have A Plan!"

CHAPTER TWENTY

Lord March was possessed of an aching head. Painful exercise of this article informed him that distress in various of his other extremities, moreover, was no less acute. His hands were bound tightly behind him, his legs tied with rope at ankle and knee—trussed up like a chicken for the pot, his lordship thought savagely.

He took stock of his surroundings, a small dark dirty chamber, the chief amenities of which were a single candle and a narrow cot. It was on this latter item that Marriot had been tossed. An attempt to achieve a sitting position having proved useless, he sank back, stared in turn at the narrow dark window, the fly-specked walls and ceiling, the closed door. Was it locked? he wondered. If only he could get his balance he might find out. Yet little would be accomplished, even were that portal opened. Marriot could hardly go hopping through a bawdy house. If only he still had his pistol, or the use of his hands and feet—if only he had heeded Nell's forebodings and not walked straight into a trap. But Nell and Mab would have seen what happened; he need only await rescue. Having come to this comforting conclusion, Lord March lay back to fret about what was taking his rescuers so long to arrive, and to listen gloomily to the sounds of raucous revelry which came through the thin walls.

Had his lordship but known it, help was on the way, by a very circuitous route that had included a spot of eavesdropping, several forays into rooms otherwise occupied, and currently an expedition up the back attic stair. Leading this expedition was a young woman dressed in sprigged muslin with a very daring décolletage. Following her was a second woman, who was prone to nervously tug at the low, square neckline

166

of her own embroidered gown. Bringing up the rear was a wispy-haired female whose attire merits less comment than her conversation, which was both vituperative and lamentably incessant, if appropriately low-pitched.

"A personal errand!" she muttered. *"Personal!* I should say it is! In a—a house of ill repute! Never did I think a member of my family—not to mention my own presence! As well as *yours,* Eleanor! What the world would say were it to learn of this—" She shuddered. "Words fail me!"

"I wish that words *might* fail you!" uncharitably retorted Lady Amabel. "If you will recall, we wanted you to wait for us outside. You refused. Therefore, if we are discovered here, you may only blame yourself for whatever scandal may ensue. But this must be the room! Look, the key is still in the lock." She grasped it and turned. The door opened. Cautiously, the ladies peered within. Their brief excursion through this house had already taught them the folly of looking where they should not—and rather more beside. But no bacchanalian scenes were being enacted in this chamber. "God bless my soul!" uttered Henrietta upon glimpsing Marriot.

Lord March did not immediately realize that his rescue was at hand, due not only to his throbbing head, but also to the dirt with which the ladies had liberally bedaubed themselves in order to add veracity to their disguise. "What the devil do *you* want?" he snapped.

"That is a fine way to talk to your knights in shining armor!" Carefully, Mab closed the door. "Unless—don't tell us you have lost your memory *again,* Marriot?"

"Your memory?" Lady March flew across the room and fetched up beside her husband on the bed. "You haven't, Marriot!"

In some astonishment, Lord March stared at his dirty-faced wife. "Nell! What the devil are you about?"

"Silly!" Lady Amabel joined Lord and Lady March on the narrow cot. "We are pulling your coals out of the fire—or trying to! Do not scowl so at me, Marriot! It

167

was not my idea to bring them along, but Nell would not permit me to come alone, and your cousin would not be left behind. I fully enter into your feelings—you think we shall all wind up in the briars—but you cannot wish to stand on bad terms with your rescuers. Oh, *bother!* I cannot untie this knot!"

"Let me try!" said Nell.

"This," announced Henrietta, outraged, "exceeds all belief! I have known all along that something very hugger-mugger was afoot, ever since Marriot said he was in Cornwall. Cornwall! You cannot deny, cousin, that you have told a great many untruths!"

"I don't deny it." Due to his awkward position—chin practically resting on his knees while the ladies struggled to untie the ropes that bound his hands—his lordship's voice was somewhat muffled. "But that was because I did not know the truth."

"*Did* not?" Eleanor sank back on her heels. "Marriot, do you now?"

Lord March turned his head. "One thing I have always known, and that is that I love you, Nell!"

"Oh, Marriot!" Her ladyship sniffled.

Neither Henrietta nor Amabel cared for this untimely digression. "*Always?*" Henrietta inquired acidly. "What about Jane?"

"Yes indeed, what *about* Jane, Marriot?" Mab struggled harder with the ropes. "Confound these things! Nell, do you think you might lend me your assistance before Marriot's assailants return?"

Looking guilty, Nell hastily resumed her allotted task. "Return?" echoed Henrietta, gingerly approaching the narrow cot. "What do you mean by that?"

Lord March regarded his cousin with keen disfavor. "Mab means Jane is a thief—oh yes, she is! And for the record I did *not* seduce her, or lend my own efforts to robbery. I recall being set upon by footpads; that much of the tale was true. Jane and her cohorts *did* take me in out of the street, for heaven knows what motive! Perhaps they thought I would make an excellent scapegoat, were they caught. As it turned out, I very nearly did for them myself, happening upon them one evening in the very act. During the resultant contretemps, I received a blow on the head."

"And your only thought was to get home to Nell!" Thrilled, Mab sighed. "*How* romantic! I wonder why the villains did not follow you—perhaps something scared them off. They must have been desperate to get back the jewels you carried away with you—but why did you smell of the stables, Marriot?"

Lord March sought a more comfortable position, an almost impossible undertaking due to the manner in which he was trussed up. "While my newfound companions were engaged in devilry, unbeknownst to me, I was engaged in honest labor. Yes, brat, I was working as a groom." His contortions allowed him a glimpse of both his wife and Lady Amabel. For the first time he realized the alterations made to their attire. "Good God!" he said.

Modestly, Lady Amabel patted her largely exposed bosom. "We had to look the part! Do not scold, Marriot; neither of us is a penny the worse for it. Oh, I wish I had kept the walking sword so that we might simply *cut* these wretched ropes—but do not despair! We shall yet contrive to get clear."

Henrietta, too long silent, deemed it time her voice was heard. "I knew I had been told a Banbury tale—several, as it turns out! I knew you weren't in Cornwall all along. No, and I knew Jane was up to no good also, traipsing about the house in the middle of the night. She *said* she was sleepwalking, but I knew better—although I did wonder if maybe the creature had set her cap for Benson since he also seemed always to be about! And now I discover—gracious! I suspected the robberies had something to do with Marriot and Lady Amabel, but I didn't suspect *what!*"

Marriot suspected he might throttle his garrulous cousin, were he still afflicted with her when his hands were set free. "Of all the crackbrained notions!" he said ungallantly. "Mab—and Nell—are involved in this business only because of me."

169

"Crackbrained, am I?" Henrietta bridled. "For your edification, Marriot, I am not so very crackbrained as you think! I know, for instance, that your wife would have liked to kiss Parrington—not that one can blame it in her, what with *you* kissing Lady Amabel!"

Eleanor looked bewildered. "I would have liked to *what?*"

Mab settled herself more comfortably. "Henrietta's gone off her hinges!" she explained. "Ma'am, I wish you would try not to act like a saphead. Especially now! Jane may appear at any moment, and we cannot untie Marriot's ropes—and we can hardly whisk him away unnoticed while he is hobbled and bound! Yet somehow we must contrive to get clear of this fix."

"Act like—oh!" Henrietta glanced about the small and dirty chamber in search of some object which she might hurl at Lady Amabel. Instead, in a far corner, she glimpsed several small furry objects complete with long tails and glittering eyes. Henrietta disliked rodents a great deal more than she disliked Lady Amabel. With a shriek, she leapt upon the bed.

"Oof!" said Mab, upon whom Henrietta had landed. *"Pray* take your elbow out of my side! What the blazes do you mean, leaping upon me—oh, never mind! Nell, do you think you might leave off being so *very* attentive to Marriot's comfort, so that we might plan?"

"You might as well," said Marriot, elevating his gaze from his wife's tempting décolletage. "I never *will* be comfortable until these accursed ropes are cut. I wonder if Jane and her cronies have yet discovered that I did not return all the jewels. Do not look so stricken, darling! We are in no immediate danger. They will dare do nothing rash with so many people around."

Irrepressible, Mab grinned. "Just think, Nell! You will be able to tell your grandchildren how it came about that you and Marriot were imprisoned in a bawdy house."

"And how I myself masqueraded as a woman of very low condition?" Eleanor looked rueful. "Thank you, Mab, but I think I must not! More to the point, let us

170

make an effort to determine how we are to remove from this place!"

"The three of you could leave easily enough," Lord March suddenly said. "And I wish you would. It can do us no good if all of us are caught."

"Piffle!" retorted Lady Amabel, though privately sharing this logical viewpoint. Logic, however, was often very dull. Moreover, Nell would not be budged from her husband's side, as made clear by the stubborn expression on her dirty face. "There is safety in numbers, is there not? To dispose of all four of us would be quite difficult."

"Dispose of—" Henrietta's uncharacteristic silence had been inspired by reflection upon her own presence in a brothel, and the uproar that would result were the story to leak out. The best of *all* her stories, and she could never tell it! "I think that I shall swoon."

"Pray do not!" Lady Amabel said immediately. "*If* you were to swoon, you'd fall on me, and I'm not up to your weight! Beside, we haven't time to waste in vaporing. Not that there is reason for it! Have you forgot I sent Fergus to Bow Street?"

"You sent Parrington—?" The temptation to swoon grew even more strong. "You wretched child! Don't you see what you've done? There'll be no way to keep this business quiet! The whole world will discover that Marriot has been mixed up in these robberies, and that all of us have been in a—a house of ill repute! We shall never again be able to hold up our heads."

"*You* may not," Eleanor retorted, having grown very tired of histrionics. "I quite frankly don't care a button for what anyone may say. They said quite enough while Marriot was merely missing. Now, no matter *what,* I no longer care."

"Darling!" Awkwardly, due to his bonds, Lord March kissed her cheek. Lady Amabel clapped her hands. "Bravo, Nell! That's the spirit! Tell *all* the old biddies they may go to the devil in a handcart!"

"As you mean to do, Lady Amabel?" Henrietta bared her teeth. "Because what is said about Eleanor and

Marriot will also be said about you—but worse! An unmarried maiden in a bawdy house—I fear that you have destroyed all your hopes of ever making a decent match."

This was a consideration that had not hitherto presented itself to Mab, and she conceded that there was some truth in Henrietta's words. That concession she made silently. "If you continue to grimace in that extraordinary manner, you'll grow positively bracket-faced!" Mab said.

"Don't tease yourself!" Marriot interrupted, as Henrietta sputtered indignantly. "I'll find some way to keep your name out of this, brat! Though the case is not so desperately bad as Henrietta paints it, you must perceive that your wisest course would be to leave."

Lady Amabel perceived nothing of the sort. "Fudge!" said she. "I doubt we *could* leave without attracting attention—just the sort of attention we would not like. Nor would you like it either, Marriot! Nell makes unusually fetching Haymarket-ware. No, we are much safer where we are—and anyway the door is locked from the inside, and I have the key." She grinned.

"I would much rather you had a knife, brat! And less great a spirit of intrigue. Not that I wish to appear ungrateful! Yes, Henrietta, we *know* you do not scruple to tell us this is a monstrous, outrageous, repugnant situation, and not at all what you are accustomed to—which will teach you the folly of poking into other people's business, because if you had not descended without invitation upon poor Nell, you would not have become personally acquainted with the inside of a bordello!"

"A—oh!" Henrietta's eyes rolled back. Only a sharp nip from Mab's fingers prevented a swoon.

"Don't fly into alt!" abjured that damsel. "I have already told you we need only wait for Fergus to fetch Bow Street. Meanwhile we can decide what story to tell when they arrive." She frowned. "I knew we would straighten out this tangle eventually! Very glad I am that we have, of course, but I am afraid that in comparison life will seem sadly flat!"

Lord March did not look like a man threatened by ennui. "I thought you said you'd locked the door, brat."

"So I did." With various squirms and wriggles, Mab fished for the key in her décolletage. "Here it is! But what are you all staring at?" She peered over her shoulder, the key held triumphantly aloft.

Boredom was not to be Lady Amabel's fate just yet. Jane stood in the doorway, the shabby valise held in one hand, and in the other a pistol trained steadily on the bed.

CHAPTER TWENTY-ONE

Lord Parrington's errand was not being speedily accomplished. His advent had precipitated a ruckus at Bow Street. "I tell you I am *not* a trifle bosky!" he said indignantly to a short and nondescript fellow with a somewhat unsettling habit of sucking in air through his teeth. "A man's life is in danger. You must come with me posthaste!"

"Posthaste, is it?" The nondescript fellow seemed to think this a good joke. "So that you may be saying how it was you put one over on old Jakes? I think not, sir! And so you may tell whoever it was put you up to it."

"Nobody put me up to it—I mean, I am telling you the truth!" In an effort to regain control of his temper, Fergus took a turn around the room. "What must I do to make you understand that the matter is urgent?"

Jakes propped his narrow shoulders against a drab and dirty wall. "I shouldn't think you *could* make me think it!" he said frankly. "But you're welcome to try."

Lord Parrington *had* been trying for several moments, both in this barren private office and in the more public regions without. Only the thought that Lady Amabel depended on him caused Fergus to persevere. As he gathered his forces for yet another attempt at explanation, the door was flung open. A familiar figure crossed the threshold. Fergus stared, temporarily bereft of speech.

Lady Katherine was not similarly afflicted. "My son!" she dramatically cried, and hobbled forward to clasp him in a maternal embrace. "I grew so worried at your continued absence that I had resolved to report *you* missing, and to offer a reward!"

"But I am not missing, Mama!" Not without difficulty, Lord Parrington disengaged himself and his walking sword from his parent, her cane and vinaigrette. "I only meant to attend the theater with Lord March's party—but there is no time now for explanations! We must persuade this person—" He indicated their host. "—to rescue March."

"Rescue?" As if to assure herself of his safety, Lady Katherine walked all around her son, eyeing him, patting his multiple-caped overcoat. "Why the deuce should March stand in need of rescue? Rather, it is *you* who should be rescued, son, from the clutches of that designing female." She glanced at the nondescript individual. "Faith, *she* should be taken into custody, methinks!"

"*No*, Mama, you may not have Lady Amabel arrested." Sternly, Fergus reminded himself of his parent's devotion and the sacrifices made on his behalf. "Since you are here—which I can*not* think suitable!— you must lend me your efforts on March's behalf."

"I must, eh?" Lady Katherine was not used to receiving even mild rebukes. "Why is that?"

Lord Parrington resumed his perambulations, which were not easily accomplished in that cramped space. "Lord March is in danger, as I have been trying to explain. Perhaps you may assist me, Mama. I was trying to tell this fellow how it was that March disappeared for all of six months. I believe Lady March even brought the matter to the attention of Bow Street."

"That is true; he *was* missing, and quite a scandal it was." The sharp words that Lady Katherine meant to bestow upon her son could wait. She sat down on a wooden chair, hands folded atop her cane. "As would be known by anyone who kept abreast of things."

Jakes was rather more abreast of things than his visitors might credit, was in that moment sincerely pitying this fine gentleman for so obviously dwelling under the hen's foot. And an obviously ill-tempered hen she was, moreover, in her Spanish hat of purple velvet turned up on one side and ornamented with a feather, and her voluminous pelisse. "I *do* know all that!" he retorted. "What's more, I know Lady March said she had no further use for the services of Bow Street. Now *you* tell me Lord March is in need of rescue. Why is that?"

If only Mab had told him how much to reveal! "I am not *entirely* certain," admitted Fergus with strict adherence to the truth, "but I *think* it had to do with stolen jewels."

"Stolen jewels!" exclaimed Jakes and Lady Katherine in the same breath. Before Fergus could explain, the former had focused an inquisitive stare on the gems which glittered at the latter's throat. "Not *my* jewels!" snapped Lady Katherine, with the assistance of her cane adapting a defensive stance. "Fergus, do explain what the deuce you are talking about!"

Since Jakes obviously did not believe him, Fergus cast about in his mind for some means by which to verify his tale. He remembered that Lady March had been draped about with jewels during her soirée—stolen jewels, as it turned out. Perhaps a description—? "A gold chain set with pearls, a parure of immense pearls, a diamond and gold breast ornament in the form of a bouquet of flowers, a bracelet with diamonds and rubies and emeralds set in enameled gold."

This recitation was greeted by a hush. "Has the boy taken leave of his senses?" Lady Katherine querulously inquired.

"I am *trying* to explain why March is in danger!" Fergus cast his parent a most unfilial glance. "Somehow he came into possession of the stolen gems. Lady March wore them at her soirée in an attempt to flush the thieves out—"

"Soirée?" Lady Katherine had recourse to her vinaigrette. "You went to that woman's soirée after I had intimated you should not? Bacchanalian scenes! Sordid little intrigues! Oh yes, I know all about it—and as if *that* were not bad enough, now you must dangle after Lady March!"

Fascinating as were these accusations, Jakes felt compelled to intervene, and not only because he feared

176

Lord Parrington would skewer his mama with the walking sword. This violent impulse, Jakes did not condemn. Had Lady Katherine been Jakes's mama, he would not have hesitated one instant. "And *did* the thieves reveal themselves?" he asked.

"I believe so." Fergus loosened his fingers on the sword. "I believe March was to meet with them tonight, on the pretext of handing over the gems. Instead he was overpowered, and dragged off. *Now* perhaps you will concede that his rescue is a matter of considerable urgency!"

"Oh, aye." Jakes did not move. "And where was his nibs dragged off *to?*"

Lord Parrington was in a fever of impatience. "To a bawdy house!" he snapped. *"Do* get a move on, man, or we will be too late." Now that he had time for reflection, Fergus doubted very much that Mab would be content to wait long out in the street. And if anything happened to his Mab—Unfortunately, the baron spoke this last thought aloud.

"Amabel!" shrieked Lady Katherine. "You didn't mention *her* before! I should have known the vixen was mixed up in this business. I think I must forbid you to have anything more to do with her, Fergus, so thoroughly have you fallen under her spell."

Lord Parrington's reaction to this stern paternal decree surprised even the baron himself. "Forbid me all you want! It makes no difference. Since I cannot please everyone, no matter *how* hard I try, I am henceforth going to please only myself." He strode toward the door. "With or without assistance, I am going to see what I may do for March!"

Warily Jakes eyed Lady Katherine, who had fallen back on the wooden chair in a most nervous and prostrated state. "I'm sorry to tell you, sir, that you *ain't!*"

What was this? Had he not just asserted his independence? Lord Parrington glanced irritably over his shoulder. As he glimpsed the pistol that had as if by magic appeared in Jakes's hand, his eyebrows rose.

"Beggin' your pardon, I'm sure, sir!" Though shaken

by the baron's haughty look, Jakes saw his duty plain. "But it's clear to me you know more than a body *should* about certain stolen sparklers. *More* than ample ground for suspicion you've given me, sir! And so, I make no doubt, the magistrates will think."

"The magistrates," echoed Fergus, thunderstruck by this intimation that he was about to be taken for a criminal offense. "You must be mad."

Unkind allegations had no power to sway Jakes from his duty. "Not a bit of it! Don't be trying to tell me now that you know nothing about this business, because you obviously do—more than Bow Street! Despite the most rigid and searching inquiries!"

"What little I know was told me by Lady March," protested Fergus. "As I have explained."

"Lady March!" moaned Lady Katherine, recovering from the shock attendant upon seeing her beloved offspring arrested before her very eyes. "The jade!"

"No, Mama, you are getting muddled; it is Mab who you are in the habit of calling names. *Not* that I intend to tolerate it another moment! As for Lady March, I am *not* dangling after her, nor do I imagine it would avail anyone to do so; she is devoted to her spouse."

Lady Katherine was not so easily quelled. "Devoted to a man who goes about embracing other females?" she inquired, archly.

"March was merely comforting Mab, she tells me; and that he's also spanked her when the occasion warranted." Fergus reflected that his own mama might have benefited from the occasional chastisement when young. "This is fair and far off! If this birdwit takes me into custody, Mama, *you* must go to March's rescue."

"*I?*" Lady Katherine's astonished expression suggested her son was the birdbrain.

Fascinating as was this conversation—Jakes would have liked to meet this Lady Amabel of whom so many interesting things were being said—it got them no further forward. "I must tell you that whatever you say to me about this matter may be used against you!" he announced after clearing his throat.

"Aha!" crowed Lady Katherine. "I knew there was something dishonest about that chit!"

Lord Parrington was growing very wearied of his mother's vaporings. "We are not talking about Lady Amabel. Rather, *we* are, but this fellow is not. *He* persists under the delusion that I know more than I have said about the jewels."

Thus referred to, Jakes felt obliged to speak. "Aye!" he said.

"I am a suspicious and dangerous character," explained Fergus to his dumbfounded parent. "And as such am about to be detained—or whatever is done to such characters. It will make a dreadful scandal, I daresay."

"Scandal?" Lady Katherine thought it might. She would never live down the disgrace, in fact. If only it might be prevented! Feeling very frustrated, she gripped her cane.

"Scandal!" repeated Lord Parrington to underscore the point; Fergus understood the workings of his parent's mind very well. "The pity is it *could* be avoided, if only this fellow could be persuaded of his error, and permit me to return to where I left March. As it is—" He shrugged. "We are likely to lose *both* March and the jewels. *I* would not care to be responsible for such a blunder, I think."

Nor, for that matter, would Jakes, who had more than a passing acquaintance with the acerbic tongue of his Chief Magistrate. But he dared not approach that worthy with such a queer tale as this. What to do? It was as Jakes pondered this weighty question that Lady Katherine made her move. She threw her arms up in the air, thrust out her feet before her, and uttered a pathetic croak. "Begod!" uttered Jakes, astonished. Pleased by the success of her dramatic debut, Lady Katherine promptly lolled out her tongue, rolled back her eyes, and allowed her head to fall forward on her chest.

"It is a seizure!" explained Lord Parrington to his appalled companion. "She has them frequently, alas.

179

Her sensibilities are very delicate. You should not have arrested me in front of her."

"How was I to know, sir? Shouldn't we do something?" Jakes was smitten with guilt.

With raised eyebrows, Lord Parrington indicated the pistol which was still pointed at his chest. Abashed, Jakes lowered it—and then things happened so quickly that he was never able to explain afterward just what had come about. To one thing, however, Jakes readily attested: Lord Parrington was very handy with his fists.

"Come along, Mama!" Fergus demanded impatiently, having with expert application of said fists laid his captor out cold on the floor. Then he appropriated Jakes's pistol. Fergus already had the walking sword, of course; but it paid to be prepared. "There is no time to waste. I would leave you behind if I did not think this fool would arrest you upon awakening—but if you cannot keep up with me, I will leave you to make your own way."

"Make my own way *where?*" inquired Lady Katherine, who had made a remarkable recovery from her fit. Briskly, she heaved herself erect. "The carriage is outside, waiting to convey me—us!—home."

"Excellent!" Lord Parrington peered cautiously into the hallway and deemed it safe. "But we are not going immediately home. Come along, Mama!"

At a faster pace than was her habit, Lady Katherine obeyed. "*Not* home?" she quavered. "Then where? I am already exhausted by the exigencies of this day. Fergus, you do not mean to try and rescue March yourself? Let the authorities deal with it!"

"I would like to very much, Mama; but you have seen for yourself that the authorities will *not*." Having safely attained the street, and discovered the carriage, Fergus bundled his parent inside. "I am afraid I must commandeer your carriage, but then I will send you home."

"*You* will send *me* home?" As result of this cavalier attitude, Lady Katherine was stricken with a palpitation in her heart. She clutched herself in the general vicinity of that organ. "Ungrateful whelp! How like a serpent's tooth!" The implications of his disrespect dawned. "You would take your own mother to a *bawdy house?*"

Fergus was discovering the joys of rebellion. "Don't worry, Mama!" he said cheerfully. "I won't insist you go in!"

"*You* won't insist—oh!" Bereft of words, Lady Katherine fell back against her seat. She did not long remain speechless, of course, and uttered countless additional words concerning selfless maternal sacrifice; but since those plaintive comments did not sway their target, they need not be presented in their entirety.

In very little time, despite the inclement weather, their destination was reached. Lady March's coachman waited where he had been instructed, and welcomed the opportunity to voice his disapproval of man and beasts left an unconscionable long time to shiver in the fog. Leaving his mama's coachman to commiserate, and his mama to indulge in a temper tantrum, Lord Parrington strode purposefully across the street.

No one sought to deny him entrance to the house, and probably would not have done so even had not he held walking sword and pistol in his hands. Fergus was a well-setup young man, after all, and obviously plump in the pocket. Of the contents of those pockets, several persons sought to relieve him, but Fergus stood steadfast. A cursory inspection of the downstairs, whilst greatly edifying, afforded him no glimpse of a familiar face. Grimly, Fergus assayed the stairs. Thereupon, he did meet someone not a stranger, a stout gentleman with a ruddy complexion and a shock of white hair—the last gentleman, in fact, Fergus had expected to see. "Good God! Sir Osbert!" he cried.

The squire, though no less surprised to happen upon his daughter's favored suitor in such exceptional surroundings, was in a much more mellow mood. Too, he had the advantage, having posted to London for the express purpose of meeting this young sprig. That the meeting should take place in a bawdy house did not disconcert him. "Zounds! You *ain't* a popinjay!" said Mab's papa genially.

CHAPTER TWENTY-TWO

Lord March gazed with displeasure at the pistol which was trained upon the bed. "This is a trifle unfriendly, Jane! After all we have been to one another, as you yourself pointed out! Having saved me turning up my toes prematurely, do you now mean to stick my spoon in the wall?"

With a grimace, Jane kicked the door shut. "I'm sure I'm civil as a nun's hen!" she snapped. "Or *would* be was you to tell me what has become of that as which I'm very wishful to get my dabbers on!"

"Wishful to—ah!" His lordship simulated enlightenment. "You refer to the gems."

"You think you've nabbed me a rum one." Wearing a grim expression, Jane approached the bed. "You and your ladies. Oh yes, I see who they are! They must have been mad as Bedlam, to follow you in here. But that's no bread-and-butter of mine! You've been behaving very scaly, and I'm very much afraid the lads'll insist on your coming to your just deserts."

Lord March's position was not so ominous as Jane made out, and well he knew it. "But not before I reveal to you where I have hidden the gems, I think. Which I do not intend to do! You must concede that the game is up, Jane."

What Jane conceded, without hesitation, was that his lordship was up to all the rigs. However, so was Jane. She glanced away from Marriot to his companions on the narrow bed. Lady Amabel was attempting unsuccessfully to heave Henrietta's inert body from atop her own. Eleanor was huddled as close as humanly possible to her husband, looking tearful and terrified. "She don't *look* like a tempersome female!" Jane remarked. "Or was that more of your taradiddles, sir?"

Lord March glanced fondly down upon his wife. "I told Jane it was because you hit me over the head that my memory was regained. You were made very angry by the intimation that Jane and I have been more than friends."

"I was?" Briefly Nell forgot her terror. "What a clanker, Marriot! As if I would ever abuse you, no matter *how* many women—don't dare to laugh at me, you wretch! You know what I mean!"

Could he have, Lord March would have embraced his wife, so delightful was her dirty face. As it was, he could only strain impotently at his bonds. "I know that I adore you, Nell!" he proclaimed, as result of which his wife embraced him.

"Not only Marriot has been telling clankers!" Mab achieved a sitting position, Henrietta sprawled across her lap. "You have been telling a fair amount of your own, Jane! We know the robberies were not Marriot's idea, as you hinted—and we know also that he didn't leave anyone floating facedown in the Thames!" She nudged his lordship. *"Don't* we, Marriot?"

"Eh? We do!" agreed Lord March. "Your cohorts served me a good turn when they set upon me, Jane. My memory *has* returned. You meant me to take the blame for your misdeeds, I conjecture; but I tumbled to your scheme and absconded with the gems."

"There's no flies on you, sir!" Jane's pistol did not waver. "And now if you please I'll just have those sparklers."

"But I do *not* please." For a gentleman in his extremely unfortunate position, Marriot was very confident. "I thought I had made that clear. You are at point-non-plus. Give it up, Jane."

"It ain't *me* as has any number of people fit to murder me!" retorted Jane. A glance at the occupants of the bed caused her to reconsider. "Or at least not so many as *you* have! I wasn't bamming you when I said the lads was wishful of carving out your liver—and I'm feeling fit to blow your brains out myself." Her unfriendly gaze moved from Marriot to his companions.

"Maybe *you* won't talk, but I fancy the lads can persuade your ladies otherwise!"

Mab fancied they might also. "Oh!" she cried. "We *have* landed in the briars, and it is all my fault!"

This lament roused Lady March from preoccupation with her mate. "Nonsense! If anyone is at fault, it is Marriot, because had he not gone to White's, and been set upon by footpads, none of us would be in this dreadful fix!" It occurred to Nell that her words smacked of censure. "*Not* that you must blame yourself, Marriot! You cannot be held accountable for your unfortunate memory! Oh, I did not mean *that* either. But Mab's intentions were the best."

Though she had lain supine—despite Lady Amabel's energetic efforts to dislodge her—through the proceedings, and had every intention of continuing inert until this abominable dilemma was resolved, Nell's assertion of Mab's innocence caused Henrietta to change her mind. "Lady Amabel's intentions were to tumble us into a bumblebath, and she has succeeded very well!" proclaimed Henrietta, heaving herself upright and glowering at Jane. "Sleepwalking, is it? You are as bad as Mab!"

"As bad as—oh!" Lady Amabel glared. "You are a devilish disagreeable female, Henrietta Dougharty! And if Fergus no longer wishes to marry me, it is largely *your* doing! He *did* wish very much to tie the knot before you told him all those taradiddles about me and Marriot—as if I *would* set my cap at a married gentleman, and one moreover who is married to my very dear friend!"

"That's as may be." Henrietta returned Mab's hostile regard. "If Parrington *had* wished to marry you so badly, I doubt anything I might have said would make a difference. But you may be sure of one thing, miss! Lady Katherine will never permit her son to marry a female who has been held prisoner in a bagnio!"

Lady Amabel did not doubt the veracity of this assertion, which endeared its utterer to her not one bit. "The devil fly with Lady Katherine!" she snapped.

The devil might fly away with the entire population of this room, herself excluded, decided Jane, who was not accustomed to having her trusty little pistol paid so little heed. Despite the fact that a gun was trained on them, Lord and Lady March gazed rapt upon one another, while Henrietta and Mab also exchanged meaningful looks—hostile and belligerent, like two pugilists preparing to square off, nose to nose. "I want to know where the sparklers are, March!"

Himself, Marriot wanted nothing more than to turn those items over at long last to Bow Street. "So you have said before. And as I have said before, I do not mean to tell you. Ergo—stalemate!"

"Stalemate, is it? I think not!" Jane's expression was very ominous, her pistol trained on Lady March. Her fell intent was obvious. Eleanor shrank back against her husband, and even Henrietta roused from her hostile contemplation of Mab. Said Henrietta, "Do something, Marriot!"

What Henrietta thought Marriot might do, trussed up like a chicken as he was, Mab could not imagine; nor in fact how anyone else might ease their peril. The situation was truly desperate. Therefore, Mab took recourse to the only remaining source of salvation. She clasped her hands together, raised her eyes heavenward, and prayed. "Lawks!" said Jane in a voice rich with scorn. And then she emitted a startled squawk, having felt in the small of her back the tip of a very sharp sword.

"Drop your pistol!" ordered Fergus, who'd entered unnoticed. "And put down that valise. For your information, I *do* still want to marry you, Mab!"

"You *do?*" Mab hopped off the crowded bed, snatched the pistol from Jane's hand. "Are you *quite* sure, Fergus? Your mama cannot think I would be the proper wife for you, and I'm not sure but what she has a point. I am *not* a very biddable female."

Lord Parrington dared look briefly away from Jane, who was giving voice to an amazing string of colorful oaths. His glance fell on the altered décolletage of Mab's

186

pretty yellow gown. With difficulty he swallowed. "I'm positive!" he said.

"Then I am very glad of it!" Mab's own gaze moved to the doorway. "Good gracious! Papa! What are *you* doing here?"

With fascination, the baronet stared upon the scene. On the bed were huddled Lord and Lady March and Henrietta Dougharty, while Fergus held at swordpoint an extremely irate female. As for his daughter—Sir Osbert also noted her plunging neckline and her dirty face. "You *are* a little zany!" he said, with disapproval. "I know you did not like me saying you were acting like a loony, but here's the proof."

"Piffle!" retorted Mab, unperturbed. "Here, Papa, take this pistol and help Fergus to guard Jane—she is very dangerous, I promise!—while I cut poor Marriot loose." So saying she snatched away the walking sword.

"Thank you, brat!" With his wife's assistance, Lord March chafed his abused extremities. "I daresay, Osbert, that you're wondering what all this is about." The baronet acknowledged that he was in fact a trifle curious. Tersely, his lordship explained.

"Good God!" Sir Osbert eyed his offspring with no little curiosity. "Ran away, did she? I made sure she'd gone to animate your wife's spirits, March. I'm sure Mab told me she had—but she ever was a mettlesome chit. A rare handful. Mab, that is, not Nell!"

"And if I am, whose fault is it?" Having cut Marriot's bonds, Mab still retained possession of the walking sword, which she now brandished beneath her parent's nose. "You never did explain how you came to be here, Papa."

Sir Osbert looked distinctly uncomfortable. "I came to town to see Parrington!" he said, lamely. "Thought I might have been a trifle harsh."

Fergus took pity on his prospective papa-in-law, whose sporting instincts were so obviously not confined to field and track. "We encountered one another en route. Has anyone any suggestion what we should do with this female? I hardly think we should remain here."

Before anyone could answer, Jane put forth her own suggestion of what her captors might do with themselves, a suggestion which led Mab to inquire whether such a thing was humanly possible, and Henrietta to almost swoon with the shock. Hard on the heels of this digression came yet another from the doorway. "There they are! Plague on't, I *told* you you had the wrong sow by the ear!" Into the room hobbled Lady Katherine, indignation personified—and furthermore handcuffed. Retorted the short fellow responsible for her humiliation, "You've told me a lot of poppycock, you and your precious son! I hope I may know a rotten fish when I smell one!" Jakes became aware of the roomful of people. "The devil! What's all this?"

"Well you may ask!" Fergus responded drily, keeping a wary eye on Jane. "On the bed there is March, who I sought to convince you was in need of assistance. Bow Street having proven uncooperative, we undertook to rescue him ourselves—with excellent results. This female—Jane!—is a thief. I believe that somewhere in this building you will find other associates of hers, and that they have been responsible for the recent series of thefts. If I might make a suggestion, those handcuffs that you have placed upon my mother would go a great deal better on Jane!"

Jakes needed time to evaluate this decidedly bizarre situation. "Thefts, is it?" he inquired.

Lady Katherine had no interest in thefts and thieves, or even in the misadventures of Lord March. Holding her cane awkwardly in her manacled hands, she hobbled across the room and halted before Mab. "You think you're going to marry my son, do you, miss?" she malevolently asked.

Lady Amabel hefted her sword into a defensive position. "Yes, I do! I am very fond of Fergus, ma'am, you see! *So* fond that I no longer mind that he is tied to your apronstrings. Or I *do* mind it, rather, but I am

188

willing to put up with you forever pulling long faces over me for his sake!"

"Put up with—!" Had not the walking sword been between them, Lady Katherine would have slapped the hussy's face. "Stab me, *I* do not mean to have a shameless twit dwelling under my own roof, so *there!*"

"Shameless twit?" echoed Fergus, his temper growing short. "I told you, Mama, that you were not to speak so of Mab. And she *will* be dwelling beneath my roof— it *is* my roof, if you will recall—because I have every intention of making her my bride!"

"I'm glad to hear it, Parrington!" Sir Osbert had been following this conversation with no little interest. "After coming upon my daughter in a bawdy house, I think she'd *better* be married! Has it occurred to anyone that we should make a push to tidy up this business?" Upon this suggestion, Lord March ceased to exchange murmured amenities with his wife and addressed himself to the baronet instead.

If it had occurred to no one else that she was in a dreadful fix, that unpalatable fact was clear to Jane. That enterprising villainess did not go down easily to defeat. Sensing everyone's preoccupation, she made a break for the door. Her dash for freedom was not successful. Down, in fact, she did go, felled by Lord Parrington with a blow from his mama's cane. Simultaneously, her prop snatched away from her, Lady Katherine tumbled onto the bed. "Oof!" said Lady March, upon whom she had sat.

Poor, *poor* Lady Katherine! Henrietta was eager to console her friend. "Is that any way to treat your mother?" she chided, casting a reproachful glance at Fergus and patting Lady Katherine's manacled hands. "Ungrateful boy!"

"You don't know the half of it!" After the recent abuse she had received, Lady Katherine greatly appreciated a sympathetic audience. "I do not scruple to tell you, Dougharty, that I am bitterly disappointed in my son. Long have I coached him in deportment, and set him a decorous example, and sacrificed and slaved—

I even assisted him to escape arrest! And to what end, I ask you? He did not even thank me! Instead he allows me to be arrested while he dangles after a girl from a bawdy house!"

"She is not *from* a bawdy house, but merely *in* it in an effort to rescue Marriot!" Henrietta pointed out. "But I know exactly what you mean! Sharp as a serpent's tooth is a thankless child!"

Lady Katherine glowered at her thankless offspring, who had flung his many-caped overcoat about Mab's shoulders and was currently applying his handkerchief to her dirty face. "I *won't* share a dwelling with that hussy, no matter *what* my son may say!" she snapped.

"No, and only a heartless monster would expect it of you!" Henrietta soothed. "You may stay under *my* roof, and welcome—although I fear you will not like it, for it is small and very damp!"

Her son's recent lack of compassion made Lady Katherine all the more receptive to this generous offer. "I shouldn't like the damp!" she retorted frankly. "Plague on't, I'm not homeless. There is always the dower house. I shall remove there, and you, Dougharty, shall go with me!"

"Thank God for that!" murmured Lord Parrington to Lady Amabel—both had been eavesdropping shamelessly. "I hope that I may make you happy, Mab. I shall certainly try very hard! But I fear I am not a very *adventurous* fellow."

Lady Amabel could not let this poor self-opinion pass. "How can you say such a thing? When you have just single-handedly rescued us? I think you have been *very* brave! As for adventure of this sort, I have had enough of it to last a lifetime." She fluttered her long eyelashes. "But there are *other* kinds of adventures, and I think we shall both enjoy them—Fergus, I would like it very much if you would kiss me again!"

Meanwhile, as Lady Katherine and Henrietta settled upon a future which was to prove of mutual advantage, and Fergus and Mab embarked upon a fervent embrace, Sir Osbert and the Marches were settling with Jakes upon what official explanation of these proceedings was best rendered to Bow Street—one, preferably, that would exclude all mention of their names. Jakes, now convinced of the facts, and additionally convinced of the glory that would be his as result of the culprits' capture, was very eager to cooperate.

"We'll bring it off safe! Sure as check!" Jakes shook his head and simultaneously sucked air through his teeth. "Here I thought I was rainbow chasing—I only followed the baron because he made off with my pistol, thinking he was right queer in the cockloft—and instead I've caught a pretty kettleful of fish." His marveling gaze fell upon Lady Amabel. "So *that's* the lass of which so many interesting things have been said!"

Lord March elevated his own fond gaze from his wife's face, and his thoughts from the various pleasurable pursuits in which they might pass their time now this mystery was cleared up, and looked instead at Mab, who was still engaged amorously with Fergus. "That reminds me, Osbert! I promised Mab I would put in a good word for Parrington."

Chuckling, Nell snuggled closer to her husband's fur-lined redingote. "I think, Marriot," she said wryly, "that you are a little late!"

And so, despite various trials and tribulations, a happy ending was contrived—save for Jane and her fellow miscreants. Yet even Jane's fate was not so dire as it might have been. Like any good villainess, Jane was not adverse to stealing a page from someone else's book. Upon official questioning, she claimed to have suffered so grievously from assault by Lady Katherine's cane that she had lost all memory, not only of stolen gems but also of how she had come to hold a lordship and three ladies captive in a house of ill repute.